THE Last Post
A NOVEL

Narendar Pani

MĀNAS

MANAS, an imprint of
EastWest Books (Madras) Pvt. Ltd.

62-A, Ormes Road, Kilpauk, Chennai 600 010.
3-5-1108, Narayanaguda, Hyderabad 500 029.
66, 'Suryashree', Shankara Park, Basavanagudi, Bangalore 560 004.

Distributors:
Rupa & Co
15, Bankim Chatterjee Street, Calcutta 700 073.
135, South Malaka, Allahabad 211 011.
PG Solanki Path, Lamington Road, Mumbai 400 007.
7/16, Ansari Road, Daryaganj, New Delhi 110 002.

© 1999 Narendar Pani

ISBN 81-86852-17-4

Price: Rs.150/-

Cover photo: Narendar Pani
Cover design: Sanka Graphics

Printed by Sri Venkatesa Printing House, Chennai 600 026.

Published by EastWest Books (Madras) Pvt. Ltd.
62-A, Ormes Road, Kilpauk, Chennai 600 010.

For
my parents

Acknowledgments

The Last Post began as a spontaneous reaction to a time when the whole of India behaved like a small town. Transforming that reaction into a novel has been a long process. The raw material first passed through the benevolent dictatorship of Jamuna, Sharat and Sarayu, who dismissed entire chapters with the shrug of a shoulder. It then went through the gentle criticism of Veena Seshadri and Rajiv Kalaswad before Subashree Krishnaswamy and Revathi Venkataraman got at the details with a persistence that, though not always adequately appreciated, was extremely rewarding.

▲ 1 ▼

As my friends will tell you, I don't like talking about myself. Even when I am asked embarrassing questions, I prefer to remain silent. All that loose talk about the way I ran the newspaper, motivated, I may add, by the pettiest of jealousies, did not get even a word in reply from me. It is not as if I couldn't have replied. As everyone knows, my command over English is excellent. An American tourist passing through Narasimhapura once told me my language was as good as that of the janitor at his university. I will not deny I was flattered at being compared to someone with such a high-sounding job in an American university. But even then I had only smiled knowingly and not used my command over the English language to talk about myself. My late wife understood my reluctance to boast so well that for the last five years of her life she never asked me a single question and her replies to my questions were monosyllabic. If you were looking for a man of few words you wouldn't have found one with fewer words than me.

It is obviously difficult for a man of my temperament to tell you a story involving so many personal details. Certainly not when I am walking down the main street of Narasimhapura in the middle of the afternoon, with a green baize tablecloth under my arm, following a bullock cart pulled by a very reluctant bullock. If you have been to Narasimhapura you will remember the main street, the one they call Mahatma Gandhi Road. I suppose it must have originally been quite wide. In fact, at the intersection around Gandhi Statue, near the bus-stop, it must be as wide as some of the roads in Bangalore. But it doesn't seem so because the front doors of the houses open right on to the main road. The shopkeepers, who have converted the front rooms of their houses into shops, have encroached at least a yard or two on to the road, and then there are the hawkers sitting a good two to three yards in front of the shops. Add to this those silly children who run blindly down the road rolling a bicycle tyre, and it is a wonder that there is any place at all for vehicles to pass. Yet vehicles do pass and some of the autorickshaws do so at a speed that leaves both drivers and pedestrians breathless. The drivers barely finish cursing the pedestrian they have nearly run over when they have to swerve sharply again in order to miss the next one. The hustle and bustle of Mahatma Gandhi Road would not have bothered my small and sprightly figure in my younger days. But with my hair having thinned, the sun has been biting into my scalp and the sweat, dripping on to my glasses. As one grows older, one also tends to be very much more careful about avoiding objects, whether they are mopeds, autorickshaws, children or the cow dung on the road.

The Last Post

And the discomfort has not been only physical. Everyone has been staring at me and sniggering. It is not that I am sensitive to these things. When you are one of the few men, forget women, who can speak English so well as to get the recognition of tourists from American universities, there will be people who are jealous. And what will jealous people do other than snigger? But the expressions on the faces of people staring at me have been more than just sniggers. There have been wide grins all round. And none of them have been friendly. The smiles of the housewives swabbing the front of their houses with cow dung paste have been full of scorn. An outsider may believe their noses are in the air because of the smell of cow dung, but everyone in Narasimhapura knows better. The little girls playing near them have been giggling with their hands over their mouths, as if I am a circus clown being paraded on the street. The shopkeepers' smiles have a he-had-it-coming look and their workers manage to look angry even when smiling. More than the physical discomfort, it is this atmosphere that has made me want to get out of the street as quickly as I can.

If I still insist on telling you about what happened during the last few days you can understand how deeply I feel about it. I had never dreamt it would end this way even in my worst nightmares. Of course, I knew a day would come when I would no longer be associated with *The Narasimhapura Post*; but that was to have been a day of glory when people would recall my contribution to *The Post*, and through it, to Narasimhapura. That was to have been a day when I would have been garlanded so profusely that I would have needed help to carry the flowers home; a day when I would have been presented an alarm clock like those given to government officials when they retire. Instead, here

The Last Post

I am walking down the street all alone in the midst of people barely trying to hide their sniggers.

You may wonder just what is it I have done that makes an entire town smirk. But I am sure that when you have heard my story, what the British would have called a sad and forlorn tale, you will agree that this is not a laughing matter.

What I have to tell you began last week. Actually, since you don't know me you may feel that I should begin earlier. You may want me to begin with the time I ran away from home in nearby Gokulpura because my father thrashed me after seeing my exam results. It is not as if I had failed or anything, it is just that he was like that. In fact, I can't remember a time when I brought my exam results home and didn't get thrashed for it. I don't remember my marks now because I left in a bit of a hurry, and it was so long ago, but I do remember that I was considered quite bright. Who knows, if I had continued studying I may have even become a major scientist and gone on to work in Bombay or Delhi, instead of spending all my life in Narasimhapura.

You have to just look at my career to understand the potential I had as a young man. The manner in which I came into journalism is something which these young so-called educated journalists of today have never experienced. How many of them began life working as a coffee boy in a little roadside shop serving a whole row of buildings on Siddappa Lane, just off Mahatma Gandhi Road, when you turn left after the silk shop? I used to serve coffee to people in so many offices.

If you are coming to Narasimhapura for the first time, you won't believe that Siddappa Lane has so many offices. After all, it is such a narrow lane that when a bullock cart enters from one side, no other cart can enter from the other side. In fact, right through the day you will find cart drivers arguing about who entered the lane first and who should make way for the other. But on both sides of this narrow lane are two-storeyed buildings with windows facing each other. The windows are so close that whenever anybody in our office wants to buy a pencil we just throw the coins into the opposite window and the pencil is thrown back. When the windows are so effective for business, how does it matter how narrow the street below is? These educated journalists may also be misled by the tiny wooden blue doors of the buildings, without realising that they lead to long corridors which lead to very large rooms.

The Narasimhapura Post was, in fact, one of the smaller offices on that lane. The board on which its name was painted in white on a black background was so small and placed so high up next to the first floor window that it could hardly be noticed. I first got to know the people in *The Post* only because they used to have so much coffee late in the night and the other boy in 'Murali's Tiffen Room' would refuse to get up when they shouted for coffee from the first floor window.

I had absolutely no idea what *The Post* was, or why it was treated with such great respect. I did not know the circumstances that had led to the setting up of this English language paper as the only newspaper in Kannada-speaking Narasimhapura. It was only some years later that I learnt how Bhimanna had faced a great deal of uncertainty about his first arrack shop; how in the years soon after the British left there was a real chance of it being closed down, all because it was near Narasimhapura's main temple.

It is not as if the arrack shop affected the temple in any way. As everyone in Narasimhapura and the nearby villages knows, the deity of the main temple is a goddess of perfect womanhood. She symbolises all that a good woman should be. As such, she has very little contact with the outside world. The temple is surrounded by a very tall compound wall painted in thick dark red and white vertical stripes. Even the area between the compound wall and the temple has always been covered with a tin roof. The only access to the temple is through the lane from Mahatma Gandhi Road that ends at the gate of the temple. The rows of wooden stalls—selling flowers and other puja items—that have lined either side of the lane for decades ensure that once you have turned into the lane there is no contact with the outside world. This was always the case. Bhimanna's shop was behind the temple and only the locals knew that the small path between two of the flower stalls actually led to the arrack shop. In its own humble way the arrack shop also helped the temple. Its existence encouraged husbands to accompany their wives to the gates of the temple. They then had something to do when their wives went in and demanded from their deity everything that a good woman would want, whether it was a son, adequate dowry for a son or even the latest gossip. Having the temple next door, along with the pictures of assorted deities on the wall of the arrack shop, also helped the customers forget their doubts about what Bhimanna put into his liquor.

The shop was important for Bhimanna too. Not only was it his first arrack shop but it had a large guaranteed clientele. Even on ordinary days nearly half of Narasimhapura's husbands, irrespective of their religion, caste or other beliefs, visited the temple. And then there was the annual festival, when for nine days every woman in Narasimhapura and its neighbouring villages prayed at the temple. Bhimanna believed that he had worked out an ideal arrangement involving himself, the people of Narasimhapura and their deity. After all, if the deity did not approve of the arrangement, would the shop have been so successful?

But in the years soon after Independence there was so much uncertainty caused by people who had nothing better to do. Like for example, Narayanappa the old freedom fighter. With freedom having been won, any sensible person would have used his record of going to jail under British rule to have gained a position in the new government. But the old idiot was a Gandhian. Not only did he not get himself a nice position, he kept looking for new things to fight for. He decided that destitute women needed his support though a lot of those women had much fitter men supporting them. He finally found that the only support he could give them—that they wanted—was to start an orphanage. Deeply disturbed that his influence did not last after the orphanage had taken care of their mistakes, Narayanappa made a great effort to appeal to other women. In keeping with his Gandhian tradition his first target was liquor, and the harm drunken husbands did to women in a family. He created an anti-arrack organisation headed by his wife and lost no opportunity to attack Bhimanna and his arrack shops. The shop near the temple was a particular favourite as it offered an opportunity to link his concern for women with the evils of arrack. But since Narayanappa was a Gandhian, Bhimanna was certain that there was no physical danger to his shop. And the fear of their drunken husbands was enough to keep many women from going against their husbands' opinion about the shop.

The trouble was that there was all this talk about the government introducing prohibition. Even if they did not fully ban the sale of liquor, the local official could decide to close down shops near a school or a temple. Bhimanna knew that the wife-beating skills of his clientele were enough to counter the Gandhian ideas of Narayanappa, but it would be a very different matter if the local official turned Gandhian. And on the day the main street was officially renamed Mahatma Gandhi Road, Bhimanna decided that he needed some access to the local government official.

This was easier said than done. The official's office-cum-residence was on the highway, some distance from the point where Mahatma Gandhi Road met the highway. It was too far from most of Narasimhapura for Bhimanna to pretend he was just passing by. And even if he was, there was little chance of him being allowed into the compound of the old colonial-style building. The official only met those he wanted to meet. And to make matters worse, he insisted on speaking only in English, a language which Bhimanna barely understood.

But Bhimanna was not one to give up easily. In his typical dogged way he pursued the official hoping to find a soft spot that could be exploited. Lesser men would have given up as the only habit, good, bad or otherwise, that the officer seemed to have was to read the English newspapers that came to Narasimhapura a day late. But Bhimanna decided that if this was the only weakness, then it was this that he would tap. He decided to set up an English newspaper in Narasimhapura.

He found two rooms on the first floor above an oil shop on Siddappa Lane. A narrow wooden staircase led to a large room, which in turn led to a very small room. He managed to buy an old run-down printing press, which he set up on one side of the large room. On the other side he placed three old steel tables in a semicircle. For the smaller room he bought a wooden desk that was large enough to cover most of the room. He also bought a green baize tablecloth that made the desk look very similar to that of the local official. There was no doubt that the small room was to be Bhimanna's office.

Bhimanna then set out to Bangalore to find a journalist who would set up a paper and run it for him. Through his contacts in the liquor trade he found an old journalist who, after having experienced years of struggle between his love of liquor and his love of writing, had allowed the former to triumph. The salary Bhimanna offered him was enough to take care of his liquor bills, and the four pages that *The Narasimhapura Post* consisted of was the most that he could concentrate on. But on those four pages he put in all the nuances of journalism that had led people, years before, to consider him a promising professional. Since his product was far better than what the official had expected from Narasimhapura, the paper soon achieved its main objective of providing Bhimanna the status to deal directly with the official.

And, surprisingly, it also became quite influential in and around Narasimhapura. The fact that it was in English did not seem to hurt, as most of the illiterate population did not mind what language they could not read. It did not really matter whether what was being read to them was the original or a translation. The translations, in fact, allowed the few persons in Narasimhapura who could read English to add or change a story according to their inclination. Like the time when Mrs.Gandhi decided to nationalise major banks. One section of the readers of *The Narasimhapura Post* were told that they could now go to a bank and take out as much money as they liked, while another section was informed that the local moneylender would now be arrested. The editor was generally too drunk to care, and *The Narasimhapura Post* soon became a paper that was all things to all people. In fact, it was believed to carry very much more than what could possibly have been fitted into four pages. Liquor finally claimed the old journalist, but by then *The Narasimhapura Post* had become a habit with its readers, listeners and those involved in producing it. At the time when I first began serving coffee to those working in *The Post*, I did not know much of this history, and, quite honestly, did not care.

And then, one day, everything changed. When Doddappa Bhimanna was getting off his 350cc motor cycle his wallet happened to fall out of his coat pocket. Or perhaps it wasn't too much of a coincidence since the stitches on the side pocket of his coat had come off. If the torn pocket was not noticeable, it was only because the rest of his coat and his once-white dhoti were not in very much better shape. By the time I ran up to the place where his wallet had fallen, he had already gone into his office. Even before I opened the wallet its weight told me it was full of money. After my trembling hands tugged at the rusted button on the wallet and opened it, I saw notes of a size I had never come across before. And so many of them. I had never seen so much money in my life.

For a moment I thought it may be a good idea to just run away with the wallet. And if you consider what has happened over the last few days it would have been the right thing to do. With all that money I could have gone into business myself, and who knows I could have even become one of those major stockbrokers in Bombay who, someone told me the other day, make more money than the prime minister.

But in those days I was young and didn't know where to go with so much money. Raghu, the other boy in the Tiffen Room, had once found a hundred rupee note and when he tried to buy a beedi with it, the police caught him and, though he refused to talk about what happened after that, everyone knew that it must have been quite terrible if it could keep Raghu from talking about it. So I quietly went up to Bhimanna and gave him his wallet.

Bhimanna was so demonstrably pleased that, for a moment, I thought the wallet must have carried much more money than I had seen. Surely someone who owned not just the little rag he called a newspaper but also all the arrack shops in the town must be used to very much more than a bunch of hundred rupee notes in a worn-out wallet. It was only later that I came to know that it was not the money that he was happy to see returned, but the wallet. He had been putting his daily collections from the arrack outlets into that wallet from the time he started selling arrack, and had got quite superstitious about it. The only time, or so the story goes, he was raided by the excise officials was the day he had forgotten his wallet and had put his daily collections into the pocket of his silk kurta. Since then he always wore a khadi kurta and used the same wallet. The return of his wallet was like his future being returned to him. In fact, when I understood how important it was, I realised that his reward of a job as an office boy in *The Narasimhapura Post* was not all that generous.

But when the offer was made I was thrilled. I was now part of a famous newspaper that everybody in Narasimhapura, and at least five villages on its outskirts, knew about. The job was also very much easier as I now only had to shout for coffee from the first floor window rather than run up the stairs with it. I spent the whole day in the outer office peeping over everybody's shoulders. I was also supposed to sleep in the same room at night, but once everyone had left I would go into Bhimanna's room, curl up on the large rosewood desk and fall asleep. The green baize tablecloth provided just the right amount of warmth that was needed in Narasimhapura's cool, but never cold, nights.

    I had so much time on my hands that I could read the paper several times over. In the beginning it was just an attempt to see if I could learn better English. After a couple of years my English became so good that I could spot proof-reading errors, especially when I went over the same story for the fourth time. At first I used to just point out the mistakes for fun. It made the proofreader's face go red when I pointed out, in front of the lady who helped with the typing, that he had allowed 'public concerns' to go as 'pubic concerns'.

    After a while though, pointing out the errors became a rather more important pastime than something done to make the typist giggle. Bhimanna had noticed that I regularly spotted proofreading errors. The frequency with which I pointed out mistakes, in fact, increased quite sharply after some pages were mysteriously torn from the office dictionary. By some strange coincidence, this happened at about the same time that I managed to buy a second-hand dictionary that I kept carefully hidden. When spotting these errors became a daily occurrence, things got quite heated at the office and one day the proofreader walked out and complained to his niece about how Bhimanna was screaming at him. His niece, who, I should have mentioned earlier, was

Bhimanna's wife, added this to a long list of complaints she had about Bhimanna not treating her family with respect. She had, she told Bhimanna every evening, always felt that her mother's brother, who had been close to them ever since his mother died, deserved better than looking for mistakes that other people made.

Bhimanna remained unfazed in the first week. In the second week he grew irritable and asked me not to point out these mistakes. In the third week, when he heard me telling the typist about the rumours that protests were being planned in front of the office because our editorial attacking a 'silly notion' of the prime minister had in print been converted into an attack on a 'silly nation', he just looked the other way. But in the fourth week when the old freedom fighter, who set up the town's defunct orphanage, had been referred to as 'a man of few wards' when the reporter insisted that he had written 'a man of few words', things got out of hand. Bhimanna had been facing a new anti-arrack campaign by a group of silly women who couldn't stop their husbands from getting drunk and instead wanted to stop everyone else from drinking. The last thing he needed was to activate Narayanappa's old antagonism on this score. Though it is doubtful that the old man's English was good enough to recognise a subtle attack on his orphanage, there was no dearth of persons who were only too willing to translate anything appearing in *The Narasimhapura Post* in a manner that would not help Bhimanna. That morning Bhimanna stormed into the office, barking at everyone all the way up the narrow wooden staircase, across the room which housed the entire staff of the paper and into the smaller room that was his office. Five minutes later the proofreader had lost his position in the paper.

Considering the anger with which it was done, the removal actually left almost everyone happy. The proofreader was made manager of Bhimanna's arrack business. This pleased Bhimanna's wife and since Bhimanna did all the managing himself, the former proofreader had little to do other than go to the office and listen to what everyone was saying about everyone else, which he did with great interest till he retired ten years later. And everybody took it for granted that I would now be in charge of looking after the proofs.

Everybody, that is, other than what's-his-name, the fellow who was the chief, and only reporter of the paper. He had been a close friend of the proofreader, with both of them sharing the same table in one corner of the office. Rumour had it that he owed his job to the proofreader.

He had known the proofreader for years, ever since they first met at the arrack shop behind the temple, when both used to escort their wives to the temple in the early years of their respective marriages. The opportunity to visit the arrack shop when their wives sought solace through more traditional means had ensured that both spent far more time around the temple than was considered normal in Narasimhapura. But soon the taunts in the arrack shop at having to rush back to their wives waiting outside the temple caught up with them, forcing them to look for alternatives.

Their combined attention then shifted to the arrack shop near the vegetable market, which allowed them to dart in for a quick visit when they bought the daily quota of vegetables, and when the mood was right they could stay longer in the firm knowledge that their wives' anger would be faced in the privacy of their house rather than in front of the temple. The common challenge that the proofreader and the reporter faced in ensuring that their visits to the arrack shop were uninterrupted strengthened the bond between them. They both saw their wives' demand for a refrigerator as a scarcely veiled attempt to stop their daily visits to the vegetable market and its arrack shop. The battle against the refrigerator was a long drawn-out one and was built on several complicated excuses including the weaknesses of specific models, the poor reputation of the dealer and, one desperate time, the tendency of all their friends who had bought refrigerators to lose their mothers-in-law within a month of the act. But the battle was finally won only years later with the advent of television, when the purchase of a colour TV before any of the neighbours pushed the refrigerator deep into the background.

In the initial stages itself the bond between the two regulars to the arrack shop was strong enough for the proofreader to mention to his niece the possibility of finding a job for a friend of his who knew so much English that he would only see the English movies that came to one of the three theatres in Narasimhapura. His niece did not give it a thought until one day during one of her regular rows with Bhimanna she did not have anything substantial to ask of him, and insisted on getting her uncle's friend a job. Bhimanna had given in, with the idea of winning some domestic peace, but soon began to realise that his new reporter had his uses. He provided a first-hand account of the customers' response to his arrack shops. And when the ladies began their anti-arrack rubbish, he wrote reports with a passion which would only have been felt by someone deeply concerned about the possibility of the closure of shops selling this essential commodity.

The relationship between Bhimanna and his reporter

though, was not always a smooth one and began to develop serious cracks after the proofreader left. For some strange reason the reporter began to believe that I was responsible for the fissures that were developing between him and Bhimanna. This was quite ridiculous, but nothing seemed to convince him that he was being irrational. When there were rumours that the reporter was being encouraged by a local politician to set up an arrack shop to compete against Bhimanna's arrack network, Bhimanna threatened to throw him out of the first floor window, and the reporter insisted that it was all my fault. How could I be blamed for merely informing Bhimanna about a rumour, a rumour that everybody in Narasimhapura was talking about, which would have reached Bhimanna sooner or later? The reporter did not also help his case by insisting that the paper should take up consumer grievances, especially when the fifth article in the series had a long list of shops where service was not up to the mark, including one of Bhimanna's arrack outlets. 'Any reasonable man,' Bhimanna told me, 'would realise that this was an attack from the competition making use of my own paper.'

It was thus only a matter of time before the reporter was asked to leave, though he once again, quite typically, sought to blame me for problems he had brought upon himself. I am sure Bhimanna would have asked the reporter to leave even if I had not told him that I saw the reporter going out with his wife. I admit that it was a mistake on my part and I had only seen the reporter with his own wife, but somehow Bhimanna mistook what I had said to mean that I had seen the reporter with his, Bhimanna's, wife. In fact, when I told Bhimanna about my mistake, the day after he fired the reporter, he laughed it off as just one of those things. But the reporter was incapable of such a broad-minded outlook and I was really quite happy he left.

I know some people said that I was happy because I was the automatic choice for the reporter's job and Bhimanna asked me to employ as a proofreader anyone I chose, but then when you are successful you have to expect people to be jealous. In any case, how could I have been absolutely sure that I would get the reporter's job? So many unexpected things can happen. After all who would have thought last week that I would be in this sorry state today?

In fact, the morning when my recent troubles started was so calm that the world appeared to be completely at peace with itself. It was one of those clear winter days when the sun is hot enough to hurt your skin when you walk on the road but not hot enough to prevent it being very pleasant in the shade. The streets were quiet early in the morning, the drivers of the five autorickshaws in Narasimhapura sat sipping glasses of tea as they discussed a particularly raunchy dance number in the latest Hindi film to come to town. The younger school children were running towards the only school in Narasimhapura while the older ones were pretending to. It was, I suppose, a very beautiful day. If, that is, you had nothing to do with *The Narasimhapura Post*. For *The Post*, the day was as dark as it was bright to the rest of the world. It was the day Bhimanna died.

▲ 2 ▼

BHIMANNA HAD SEEMED QUITE WELL THE PREVIOUS NIGHT, when he had come to the office on one of his evening rounds that had become a habit. Over the years his visits during the day had become quite irregular. His arrack business had grown, and he had also bought a tea-shop which he later expanded into a restaurant and then into the town's largest hotel, so the few hundred readers of *The Narasimhapura Post* mattered less to him. He treated the ownership of the paper more as a matter of prestige, just like his insisting that his son should study only in Bombay. Bhimanna did more things as a matter of prestige than as a matter of economics.

I sometimes wonder whether he retained the paper simply because it was in English, a language he always looked up to despite his continuous digs at English-speaking visitors like the local medical representative. After a few years he did not seem to care what I did in the paper as long as the losses grew at only a reasonable pace, and all that his wife sent across was published. I ensured that his interest in the paper did not grow beyond this level by keeping it out of trouble without making it so dull as to lose its steady, and what I consider, respectably large, readership. This was not very difficult as long as one kept the focus on people who were interesting but not powerful enough to cause trouble. And as Narasimhapura had grown, there were quite a few such people.

The anti-arrack movement was now being led by a rather pretty, spunky little girl who had come in from Bangalore to 'work with the masses'. She also had a nice name, Savitri Rao, though I believe those boys, who come in a car to see her on some weekends, call her 'Sati'. I first met her a couple of years before Bhimanna died, soon after she arrived in Narasimhapura. She had come to the office, climbing warily up the narrow wooden staircase spattered with oil, to issue a statement for the anti-arrack movement. The very idea of a representative of the anti-arrack movement expecting Bhimanna's paper to get one of their silly statements published sent everyone in the office into giggles. But I could see the girl really expected it to be done. I couldn't help smiling but I certainly didn't want to laugh her out of the office. Pretty women were not a common sight in Narasimhapura, and she certainly was one, especially when she, quite literally, let her hair down. The fact that she was quite petite made her hair seem even longer. Her upturned nose and her high cheeks had turned red as she was clearly not used to walking in the sun. The starched white cotton sari she wore could not hide, and perhaps was not meant to hide, her rather startling figure. The sari was worn low, revealing a waist that was even better shaped than those of the women in the calendars in Bhimanna's liquor shops. I looked at her for a moment, admiringly. As she slowly realised that the others in the room were laughing at her she began to blush, which made her look even more beautiful. I then walked up to her and put my arm around her shoulders. But she ducked under it and went quickly to the other corner of the room.

I was quite upset at her behaviour. I was, mind you, just putting a fatherly arm around her; anyone could see that. As if I did not know how such girls behaved in Bangalore. Who was she trying to fool, with all those boys coming to visit her on the very first weekend she was in town? But I am not a man to take such things to heart. I just told her the paper could not publish her anti-arrack material since it was the policy of the paper not to support divisive forces. She was evidently not very intelligent because she kept asking me to explain how the anti-arrack movement was divisive.

She said in that shrill voice of hers, 'I can understand if we were communal or casteist. But the anti-arrack movement is a completely secular movement. If you can point out one action of ours that is either casteist or communal I will resign.'

'Well, casteism and communalism are not the only divisive forces,' I told her. 'Any movement which divides society is divisive and you are dividing society by turning the non-drinkers against the drinkers.'

I would have thought that was obvious to anybody. Makes you wonder what they teach them in schools and colleges these days. 'I have never heard such rubbish in my life,' she snapped. With a sudden about-turn that caused her sweet-smelling black hair to brush against my nose, she walked out. And though she rarely came back to the office, I remained quite fond of her.

My fondness for her may have also had something to do with the fact that she was a far greater asset to the paper than she realised. As things turned out we were, in fact, rather lucky that she saw the paper as one of the 'instruments of oppression' in the town. After we refused to publish her little nonsense she organised women to sit in a dharna in front of the office. With Siddappa Lane being as narrow as it was, it did not take many women sitting in dharna to block it completely. This gave us all the publicity we needed in a small town. Then, there was the added benefit—any rude remark against this little girl gained us the immediate support of Krishnappa, the local politician and Narayanappa's grandson, who had never forgiven Savitri for taking away the leadership of the old anti-arrack movement from the women in his family. And since she would invariably follow an attack on her anti-arrack movement with a dharna in front of our office, we regularly published such pieces whenever we felt we needed publicity.

When Bhimanna realised I could keep his paper going without affecting, if not actually assisting, his arrack and hotel business he began to come to the office less regularly, soon dropping his morning visits altogether. In the evenings too he came mainly to catch up with the gossip, and as he grew older he preferred his gossip to be very much more spicy and very much less related to the truth. The evening before he died had followed the normal pattern. He had been quite interested when I gave him the gossip about some of the better looking women in Narasimhapura, which I had, as usual, spiced up quite considerably. But after I had finished providing him his daily dose of gossip he seemed in no hurry to leave. He stayed on, chatting about his son. For the first time he actually told me, in so many words, that his son would take over the paper after him. I nodded absently as it was generally assumed this would be the case. In fact, his son used to come to the office quite regularly when he was in Narasimhapura, though he did not get directly involved in the paper; he had studied in Bombay and his main interest in life seemed to be working out ways to get back to the big city. When Bhimanna repeated that he had left the paper to his son, I still did not pay too much attention as he had developed a habit in his later years of repeating whatever he said, as if he could not remember whether he had said it earlier. I remember wondering whether this little reference to his son was to become a part of the daily ritual after the gossip. But that was not to be. Early the next morning I was woken up by the office boy banging at the door of my house to inform me that Bhimanna had passed away in his sleep.

It took a while for the news to sink in. And when it did, I did feel a deep sense of loss. I had felt like that only once before when Lucy died. She had been a constant companion for over twelve years, ever since I had brought her back home with me from Bangalore. My wife had naturally objected to my bringing Lucy to stay with us. But I had ignored the objections as my relationship with my wife had by then become somewhat like one between a brother and a sister. And I never regretted it, as Lucy remained devoted to me. She would always wait up for me no matter how late I was at the office. She would not touch her food until I had eaten my dinner. When I stroked her soft hair she would curl up against me. She never once refused to do anything that I wanted her to do. I know a lot of people were surprised at how close I was to her and how upset I was when she died. To them she was just another pomeranian. And I suppose one should not get too attached to a dog. But that was the way it was. To tell you the truth I felt more depressed when Lucy died than when my wife died.

Do not get me wrong. I was a very good husband. I used to give my wife enough money to run the house. I used to buy her saris for all the festivals, as well as her birthday. I also never blamed her for being childless, though I had really wanted a son. I was even progressive enough to allow her to work in the school, as she was educated. In fact, I was the one who insisted that she should take up a full-time job, as she had to in any case finish the cooking and all the housework before nine o'clock in the morning and she could cook for the evening and wash the clothes after she came back from work. It was I who convinced her that her idea of a part-time job would only strengthen the old-fashioned view that a woman could not do a full-time job. But she never appreciated all this. She used to be quite sullen and every holiday she wanted to go back to her father's place. And later, when I got her father to convince her not to keep going back to his place, she would spend long hours at the temple. So much so that when she died the other ladies who went to the temple knew more about her illness than I did. But I did not hold any of this against her. Till the end I kept giving her the money and the saris as I used to in the beginning. And though I did feel sad when she passed away, I still remember the first thought that came to my mind was, who would do the cooking now.

With Bhimanna it was different. I could never forget that though I had achieved everything due to my own hard work, he had given me the opportunity. He had also been a reassuring factor all these years. Despite all the independence I had gained in running *The Narasimhapura Post*, Bhimanna was always there. He had his little irritating habits, particularly his insistence that everyone in the office should stand up and bow low when he entered the room, but he had always treated me well. I knew he had a cruel streak in him which was in evidence when he went about destroying the local lawyer, first by threatening his witnesses and later by threatening even his clients, only because he married a woman who had scorned Bhimanna; but I was never subjected to this side of his character. He had been a father figure to me and I had treated him as such even when he was a frail old man in his eighties.

Once the shock of realising Bhimanna was no more began to fade, other more worrying thoughts came to mind. *The Narasimhapura Post* would I suppose, as Bhimanna said, pass on to his son, the boy he had adopted when he was nearly fifty. The news of Bhimanna suddenly picking up a boy from the town's orphanage had surprised many in Narasimhapura who knew the background from which most of the children in the orphanage came. Initially most of us believed it was just a gesture to gain the support of Narayanappa. The old freedom fighter was quite soft on anyone who adopted a child from his orphanage, and over the years his antagonism to Bhimanna's arrack shops did lose its sting. But Bhimanna used to bring the child regularly to the office. No one could have imagined that people as conscious of their caste as Bhimanna and his wife were, would actually be so warm to a boy from the orphanage. But there it was. They called him Gopalakrishna, after Bhimanna's father, and as the boy grew there was nothing that Bhimanna would not do for him, sending him to the best school in Bangalore and then to a college in Bombay.

As the boy became more and more educated he seemed to lose all his manners. When he was still in Narasimhapura he would call me the Kannada equivalent of 'uncle'. When he went to school, and his English became better than his Kannada, he would call me 'uncle'. By the time he reached college it was 'Mr. Rangarajan'. And when he came back to Narasimhapura after his education to be nominally in charge of his father's business, it became just 'Rangarajan'. I suppose I was lucky it did not become 'Ranga'. I couldn't help wondering what he would now want to do with *The Narasimhapura Post*, or for that matter, with me.

It was this thought that was at the back of my mind as I put on a dhoti, instead of my usual trousers, and rushed to Bhimanna's place. It took me a while to get there as the house was some distance away, on the highway. Ever since he had first wooed the local official, Bhimanna had considered a large house on the highway as the ultimate sign of status in Narasimhapura. And ten years ago he had finally built that large house. He had paid a great deal of personal attention to building it and was very proud of the result. Indeed, he was so worried that everyone passing on the highway would cast evil eyes on it that he built a high compound wall with tall steel-sheet gates. Every inch of the compound between the wall and the house was cemented. The verandah had tall black granite pillars. Each wall of every room, as well as the roof, was painted in a different colour. Bhimanna was particularly proud of his choice of colours for the outer wall, which was covered with slanted maroon and orange stripes. By the time I got there there was already a small crowd between the gate and the house. A group of them were sitting on the polished stone steps of the verandah talking in hushed tones. The number of people who had gathered so early in the morning did not surprise me as over the years Bhimanna had built a rather large circle of acquaintances who were indebted to him, financially or otherwise. Nor was I surprised to find when I got to the steps that, though their tone was solemn enough, they were discussing the same raunchy dance number that was a hit with the autorickshaw drivers. Bhimanna had died at an age when the sorrow of his passing did not have the sharpness of the unexpected. I slowly made my way through the crowd to the green and orange room to pay my last respects to Bhimanna's body which was laid out on a mat and covered with flowers. I also offered Gopalakrishna any help his family may have needed. But that was a mere formality. As close as I had been to Bhimanna, he had, for some unknown reason, never encouraged me to get very close to his family. My role was confined to *The Narasimhapura Post* and I knew I would be better off returning to *The Post* to ensure that the next day's issue would be a tribute to Bhimanna. I tried to put all the nagging doubts about the future out of my mind as I concentrated on what the front page carrying the news of Bhimanna's death would look like. As I walked slowly back to *The Post* I shut out from my mind the sounds of heavy traffic on the highway and the cycle bells and the curses of the autorickshaw drivers. These things are unavoidable when walking down Mahatma Gandhi Road in the morning. By the time I reached *The Post* and sat at my desk the picture of the next day's edition was clearly imprinted in my mind. It had to have a black border that was thick enough to draw the attention of even the most casual passer-by, but it could not be so thick as to get smudged in the printing. I was trying to make up my mind on whether it should be half an inch thick or three-quarters of an inch, when a squeaky voice from the door startled me. 'What do we do about the soccer match, Sir?'

What an idiot, I thought for the umpteenth time as I looked up at the young man who uttered these callous words. He was over six feet tall. His long hair was combed back. He was wearing his usual white khadi pyjamas with his off-white khadi kurta, both washed clean but not ironed. The bag was, as usual, full and slung on his right shoulder. Ever since I had first seen him two years ago he had always been dressed like this, as if this was the uniform for the only reporter in a small town paper.

The fact that he was the reporter of *The Narasimhapura Post* was itself the result of unfortunate circumstances. I had always maintained that I was, at fifty-eight, still quite fit and did not require the assistance of a reporter. But Gopalakrishna insisted that I did, with a vehemence that told me he had already made up his mind about who it should be. When one day he told me, in front of Bhimanna, about a friend of his from Bombay who had an M.A. in History and wanted to work in a small town because he was committed to the cause of the less privileged of our society, I instantly objected. I pointed out that such a boy would not understand how our town worked. And my apprehensions were borne out the very next day when he came to the office and introduced himself as 'Puttaswamy Krishna, or Putty for short'. I could see that Bhimanna was quite startled and it took a while before we could explain to him that Puttyforshort was not a new caste name. But Gopalakrishna had made up his mind, and Bhimanna always gave him what he wanted. As a result I was saddled with a reporter who at a time when Bhimanna had just died could only think of a football match, and didn't even have the sense to call it football.

'What do we do about the soccer match, sir?,' he repeated.

'I heard you,' I told him curtly.

'I will be covering it.'

'Why, have I asked you to cover it? Has anybody even come to the office and asked us to cover it?'

'Yes, the municipal president had come and asked me to cover it.'

I was now furious. 'Asked you, asked you...who is he to ask you? Is he now running this paper, or am I?'

'Well sir, since you were not here I agreed to cover it.'

'And who are you to agree to cover it? I don't think we need to cover it at all. So now you can go and tell him you disagreed to cover it.'

'But sir, the match is important for Narasimhapura. After all it is not just another soccer match.'

This was too much. Did I require this stupid young fellow to tell me what was important in Narasimhapura? Of course I knew that this was not just another football match. It was a match between the Barkis and the Old Residents of Narasimhapura, and all the traditional enmity was bound to come to the surface.

The enmity can be traced back several decades. The Barkis were then a small group who had come to Narasimhapura from a neighbouring region because a severe drought made the cultivation of their small plots of dry land unviable. They had initially set up huts on the empty piece of land near the temple where the cows grazed. Since the arrack shop was behind the temple they began to earn a living by making and selling vade to the customers of the arrack shop. They, in fact, got their name from this activity as Bar-ki meant 'of the bar' in Narasimhapura's version of Hindi. As Bhimanna's business grew and the number of arrack shops increased so did the number of little stalls selling vade. As the stalls moved away from the temple, they widened the choice of eatables they offered to include boiled eggs and later, even meat balls. And as their businesses grew so did the number of Barkis who gave up their land to come to Narasimhapura.

The growth of this community did not initially cause any problem. They seemed to fit in quite easily with the rest of Narasimhapura, their shops providing a sort of supplement to the arrack trade. Culturally too there were no real tensions. They were quite similar to the people of Narasimhapura. They spoke the same language, though their dialect was different. Their form of worship was also similar, except that they worshipped a god while the deity in Narasimhapura's main temple was a goddess. Their physical features too were not very different, and most people who didn't belong to Narasimhapura could not make out the difference between a Barki and an old resident of Narasimhapura. The Barkis also did little initially to make the Old Residents feel uneasy. They built their temple close to, but at a respectable distance away from Narasimhapura's main temple. It was on a narrow lane between two flower shops on the road in front of the main temple. But it was a good ten minutes walk from the main temple. Their temple was also very much more modest in size and design than the main temple. The Barkis seemed to acknowledge that they were, status-wise, a notch below the Old Residents of Narasimhapura.

As a new generation of Narasimhapura-born Barkis began to grow up they branched out into new activities.

The Last Post

Some years ago a couple of the Barki boys had set up a cycle shop towards the less busy end of Mahatma Gandhi Road. There were some disputes about the hiring of cycles, but they were not serious.

And then something happened that changed everything in Narasimhapura. When the Barkis had decided to leave agriculture they had not been able to sell their land as it was not considered cultivable. They continued to own the land, even though they rarely visited their native place. The sentimental value of the land declined, becoming virtually non-existent for the younger generation. Then news came that a major paper manufacturer had set up a factory near their land. He needed to generate a steady supply of eucalyptus for his factory. And since this tree could evidently grow anywhere, he offered to buy the Barkis' land. The Barkis, who had long ago forgotten that their land had any economic value, suddenly received a windfall.

And they made no attempt to hide it.

The cycle shop, almost overnight, became a moped and motorcycle garage. Another one was set up to cater to the vehicles passing on the highway. Then they even started a school, which was supposed to be for everybody but was actually full of Barki boys. These boys could be seen zooming up and down on their motorcycles, disturbing the peace of Narasimhapura. As the garage on the highway grew bigger, and there were more Barki boys with motorcycles, they began to get on the nerves of the traditionally quiet and tolerant residents of Narasimhapura. Though the Barkis were only a small minority in the town you could see them everywhere because our boys were so timid and well brought up that they rarely loafed around. Now they had gone so far as to actually challenge the old Government High

School, Narasimhapura, to a football match. And as was typical of the uncultured Barkis they did not even have the courtesy to come and meet me and request me to have the match covered. Instead, they had got the municipal president to talk to that idiot of a reporter. If they thought that was enough to get the match covered, I would show them. Mind you, I had nothing against Barkis. Some of my best friends were Barkis. But how much more could the normally tolerant people of Narasimhapura tolerate?

'The match will not be covered,' I told Puttaswamy.

'Why?' he had the temerity to ask me.

'I don't have to tell you why, I don't want it covered, that is all.'

'But the paper has always had a very good relationship with the Barkis.'

There he was again telling me about the paper itself. As if I didn't know about the relationship the paper had with the Barkis. It was cordial because they supplemented Bhimanna's arrack business. But I was sure Bhimanna would not have approved of the behaviour of the younger Barkis towards the paper, especially now that the garage owners were said to be starting their own hotel to compete with Bhimanna's.

'There is no question about it,' I told him firmly, 'the football match will not be covered.'

'But Gopi, I mean Mr. Gopalakrishna, has already told me to go ahead and cover it.'

There it was. Out in the open. Bhimanna had not even been cremated and it was already being made clear that my writ will no longer run.

Well, running *The Narasimhapura Post* was not as simple a job as they thought it was. If they wanted to take the decisions without knowing how to run it, let them. They would also have to face the consequences. And the consequences I was sure would be quite painful, even if I had to die to make them so.

The reactions to the edition announcing the passing away of Bhimanna were entirely along expected lines. I was woken up early in the morning by Gopalakrishna banging on my door. He was panting hard and must have run all the way from the highway, down the full length of Mahatma Gandhi Road to the mud lane where I had built a house large enough to suit my stature. From the condition of his clothes it was clear that he had not taken the care that is necessary when hurrying along a mud lane. Fortunately, he was back to wearing his blue jeans and a bright yellow T-shirt, after having worn a white pyjama and kurta the whole of the previous day as a mark of respect to his father. But even his dark denim jeans could not hide the mud they had collected on the way. And parts of his T-shirt were soaked in sweat. As he took a few moments to catch his breath, it was obvious that he was very angry. His hair was dishevelled and the expression on his face made it clear that anger had overtaken any sorrow he may have felt over his father's passing away.

'My mother would like to know,' he virtually screamed, 'why the paper did not devote the full front page to my father. Did he not run this paper for over half a century? And you have gone and put a football match story next to the news of his passing away. Have you forgotten my father already?'

'Calm down,' I told him. 'You will get nothing by

shouting. I had intended to devote not just a whole page but the entire issue of the paper to your father. But Puttaswamy told me that you thought the football match was very important, so I gave it equal importance.'

'I didn't mean it that way,' he said, his anger turning into defensiveness with a swiftness I would have found difficult to understand, had I not known just how formidable his task would now be to explain to his mother that he was responsible for the lack of importance being given to his father's death. Especially after I had told her my version of her son's role.

Gopalakrishna had just stood up to leave when Puttaswamy came rushing in. The mud lane outside had not discriminated between Puttaswamy and Gopalakrishna, but on Puttaswamy's pyjama and kurta it had a more startling effect. He looked very much like the actor who played the role of the beggar in a production of the drama company that had recently performed in one of the villages near Narasimhapura. Gopalakrishna gave him one nasty glare and stomped out of the house. It was now Puttaswamy's turn to sputter. 'You have got my story all wrong. I did not write all that you have put under my by-line. I had focused primarily on the soccer match and had just mentioned that there was a minor skirmish outside between a Barki boy and a couple of boys belonging to the Government High School. But in what you have published there is no mention of the match. You have expanded the skirmish into the main story, making it look like a riot. People are talking about it all over town. They think I am just another rabble-rouser trying to create trouble. In the tea-shop someone was saying I had been bribed by people who did not want peace in Narasimhapura. If I had wanted money would I have come to this little town? You think I could not have got a job in the city? I came here because Gopalakrishna told me about this little paper in a small town which could influence people. I came here to help spread all the knowledge I have.'

I looked at the boy disdainfully. Knowledge, indeed. I had never met anybody who knew less about what mattered. He kept talking about Marks and Angles and some other such names, as if they knew anything at all about Narasimhapura. In some odd way I felt sorry for the boy's stupidity, and when I spoke, the words came out much softer than I usually manage when speaking to the fool.

'I don't have to explain what I put in the paper to you. But I may as well, since I don't agree with it either. You seem to have forgotten that I would not have covered it if it hadn't been for you. You were the one who said that it was not the football match but the conflict between the Barkis and the Old Residents of Narasimhapura that was important. Since that was your argument I elaborated on the conflict to make sure the report captured all that you felt.'

His jaw fell, his shoulders shrank and he looked generally so pitiable that I had to keep myself from laughing.

The most important visitor was waiting for me when I reached the office. The local sub-inspector of police, Nanjappa, had a copy of the paper before him as he sat on my chair, with his feet on the table. He was the only person, now that Bhimanna was dead, who dared to walk straight into the office and sit on my chair. The first time he walked straight behind the table and eased his short stocky frame into that chair, everybody in the office was surprised. I thought he may have taken the wrong chair by mistake and said so. But he had pretended not to hear. Over the last year others in Narasimhapura had confirmed that he had a habit of throwing his weight around. The fact that he had been posted to Narasimhapura, despite having paid a large bribe for a more lucrative posting, had only made him more abrasive. And his entire manner was quite aggressive as he crossed his legs, leaned back in my chair, and looked at me.

'Rangarajan, I don't understand this. Your paper has always tried to keep a peaceful atmosphere in Narasimhapura. But this report has somehow managed to hurt the feelings of both the Barkis as well as the Old Residents. Both sides have complained to me already. There is also some tension over the fight now, though last evening it was almost forgotten. I can't believe that you, with all your experience, could have done this.'

It was now my turn to look pitiable.

'What to do, inspector,' I told him mournfully. 'It is all in my karma. I warned the boys against publishing a story on the football match. But they insisted that it be covered.'

'Well, because of your old record, I am not taking action this time. But tell your reporter that if he writes another report of this kind I will put him behind bars.'

'I will do that, inspector. But these boys just don't listen. Could you call him to the station and tell him what you think in no uncertain terms?'

I had to keep myself from smiling as I thought of Puttaswamy with his funny English trying to explain his case to the sub-inspector who had great faith in the use of fear to maintain law and order.

▲ 3 ▼

THE NEXT MORNING I WOKE UP FEELING QUITE RELAXED. THE tensions and doubts created by Bhimanna's death had receded. After the mess that Gopalakrishna and Puttaswamy had made of *The Narasimhapura Post* the day after the old man's death, I was sure that I would be needed more than ever before. All I had to do was ensure that I did not push Gopalakrishna too far by gloating over his predicament. And, just to make sure that there were no doubts on his side, I also resolved to treat him with the same kind of subservient behaviour that I had reserved for Bhimanna. Considering that I had been quite rude to the boy in the past I was sure that such behaviour would melt him. As I always do when I am relaxed, I dressed with greater care than usual. I wore a clean white terrycotton pant, a white kurta and white leather slippers. The top two buttons of my kurta were kept open so that the gold chain round my neck was clearly visible. I could now look forward to Gopalakrishna's visit at noon.

Once I stepped outside my gate it was apparent that things were not normal. I didn't pay too much attention to it immediately, as I was concentrating on not getting my white slippers too muddy from the slush on the lane outside my house. But as soon as I turned into Mahatma Gandhi Road it was clear that the tension generated by yesterday's paper had not completely vanished. The main street was quite deserted, if you did not count the policemen. There were more policemen than I had ever seen before in Narasimhapura. There were policemen in a van parked in front of the tea-shop; there were two policemen sitting on the steps of Jain's Cloth Store with a rifle between them; and small groups of policemen were strolling down Mahatma Gandhi Road, and every other street, trying to look authoritative in what were obviously unfamiliar surroundings. I heard later that ten vanloads of policemen had been rushed in from Bangalore on the advice of the local administration. Ever since the MLA from the neighbouring constituency had become a minister he had kept sending in vanloads of policemen at the slightest pretext, just to show his newly acquired power. And the IAS officer who had just been posted to Narasimhapura was so new that he would send for reinforcements if two bulls had a fight on one of the side roads. I couldn't help feeling that the tension would have been much less if there weren't so many policemen with their .303 rifles around. But then these were matters that did not concern me. If they wanted to call out the army in Narasimhapura, how was it my business? As far as I was concerned the insecurity that I had felt the previous day had completely disappeared. The thought of having organised a smooth transition from Bhimanna's reign to that of his son, made me feel quite light-headed. I had to wipe the smile off my face as I entered the office, so that people did not think my behaviour unusual.

Not that there was anybody in the office at nine in the morning to notice such things. The only person in at that hour was my secretary-cum-office-typist-cum-advertising-clerk, Rajalakshmi. And Rajalakshmi rarely noticed anything, usual or unusual. All the more so on days when she was convinced her husband was having an affair. Over the last ten years that she had been in the office I had only seen her in two moods. When she believed that her husband was having an affair she would sit staring at the antique typewriter, elbows on the table, and plump cheeks resting on her palms. And when she realised that he was not, which was usually a week later, she would lean back on the chair stretching as far as her short, round body allowed her to, staring at a film magazine with a smile that split her face in two. This was a day for staring at the typewriter.

When she was in this mood we followed a strict ritual. I would go across and sit down on my chair, as if I had not noticed her. She would keep staring at the typewriter, waiting for me to ask her why she was so gloomy. She would then blink back her tears, come over to my table, noisily pull back the foldable steel chair in front of it, plonk herself down and begin her tale of woe, invariably with the words, 'I suppose it is all my karma.'

'I suppose it is all my karma,' she said that day, waddling across to my table even before I finished asking her, with the necessary concern, why she was so gloomy. Her body had clearly seen slimmer days, but she was still quite pleasant looking. Her plump cheeks had a touch of freshness about them that belied her forty summers. She had had an expression of innocence when I had first employed her ten years ago which I thought had made her look much younger than her thirty years. Today, ten years, three children and a thousand doubts about her husband later, she had still not lost that overwhelming air of innocence.

'I suppose it is all my karma,' she repeated as I absorbed the calmness that her innocence always radiated. I rearranged the already neat stack of papers on my table, leaned back and listened. 'I really don't know what he sees in her. I would not even have looked at her if it wasn't for the strong perfume. She looks like a little mouse. She is so thin that if my little finger touched her she would fall down. She is so short that any man would have to keep looking at the ground to make sure he doesn't trip over her. It is not as if her face is very beautiful either. Her nose is like a pomeranian's. Her voice is so shrill that whoever she marries should be given a bottle of ear-drops as a wedding present. She may be fair, but as if colour is everything. If she had to work like me in the kitchen, I would like to see how fair she remains.'

As usual I didn't have a clue as to who she was talking about, but she was bound to tell me sooner or later. When she was in this mood I let her talk and only rushed her by asking questions if I was busy. I had plenty of time now. Gopalakrishna was only expected at around noon, and it was still only a half past nine. So I settled back in my chair listening to her continuous prattle, thinking, as always, how beautiful she once must have been.

Her tirade against the woman in question went on for the next half-hour covering the woman's lack of taste as was evident in her choice of saris, her preference for those stick-on bindis of odd shapes that no respectable woman would wear, her high-heeled slippers adding to the potholes on

Narasimhapura's roads and her use of wooden bangles and earrings, 'as if she was a tribal', in that order. I was wondering whether I should prod her into getting on with her story, when she mercifully moved into the second stage of her complaint: the self-pitying I-never-thought-she-would-do-this-to-me stage.

'It is not as if I have ever done anything to her. In fact, I hardly know her. The few times I have seen her we have never spoken. It is not as if I have met her socially. The only times I have seen her have been either on the road or in this office. When she came here with that silly petition against Bhimanna and wanted us to publish it, I was the only one who did not laugh. Even the other day when both of us were waiting for an autorickshaw, I let her take the first one because she said she was in a hurry. And this is what I get in return. I suppose I should have expected this from someone who keeps asking women to fight for their rights against their husbands. I suppose she feels she can get her hands on the husbands once their wives leave them.'

I must confess I was a bit surprised. I just did not even for a moment during her long diatribe think that she could have been talking of Savitri Rao. No one in their right senses could believe that Savitri would have had anything to do with Rajalakshmi's husband. While, in keeping with Rajalakshmi's usual stories, this was also unlikely to be true, I did not think even Rajalakshmi's vivid imagination would have gone so far as to link the attractive political worker with her businessman husband. In fact her husband had every reason to dislike Savitri. He was a locally educated boy, well dressed, with his hair always oiled and combed, who had always felt uneasy with westernised, sophisticated women who, I read somewhere, carefully cultivated their careless looks. I remember once he had come rushing to me because Savitri had said 'Howdy' to him while he was crossing the street; he had thought it was an insult. And, more than anything else, it did not suit his business interests to be on the same side as, let alone get emotionally involved with, Savitri.

Mohan, Rajalakshmi's husband, was one of those boys Narasimhapura was very proud of. He had studied in the local school on Mahatma Gandhi Road like all other boys of his generation. Like them he used to run to school in the morning, rolling a cycle tyre with a stick in one hand, books in the other. On the way back from school he too had tried to knock tamarind off the trees by throwing stones stored in the pockets of his khaki shorts. And like all the others he was quite quick on his bare feet when the stones missed the tamarind and broke something else. But Mohan was also very different from the others. He passed his exams every year. In his final year at school, he got a second class, something that nobody in Narasimhapura had ever done before. That he had managed to do so with only the limited financial support that his coffee shop-owning father could provide, had added lustre to his success. The fact that he would keep reading his school books in between serving coffee at his father's shop had got all those who visited the shop quite involved in his progress. When he finished school it was clear that his father would not be able to send him to college in Bangalore. But everyone also felt that he deserved to do better than wait to inherit his father's coffee shop. It was then that Narayanappa, the old freedom fighter, stepped in.

Narayanappa's orphanage was going through a

particularly bad phase. His son had dutifully followed in his father's footsteps and called himself a politician though everyone knew he did not share any of his father's commitment to social issues. His father tried to instil a sense of responsibility in him by getting him married to a nice young girl from a village just far enough not to have heard of the boy's reputation. It did not take long for the wide-eyed excitement in the girl's eyes to turn into deep sorrow. By the time their son Krishnappa was born, husband and wife were barely talking to each other. Though she stayed on to look after Narayanappa, her husband rarely came home.

In a second attempt to instil responsibility in his wayward son, Narayanappa put him in charge of the orphanage. He told his daughter-in-law, once he learns to take care of other people's children, how can he ignore his own son?

Unfortunately for Narayanappa, his son did not go through the first step of taking care of other people's children. He used the office of the orphanage, with its sprawling building surrounded by trees and a large compound just off the highway before you enter Narasimhapura, to meet his friends. Soon stories about his drunken parties at the secluded orphanage were the regular fare at the local tea-shop, but the interest that greeted the first stories rapidly slid into boredom as the excesses of the parties became repetitive. It was only when stories of women screaming at night reached Narayanappa's ears that he felt some measure of control was necessary. And his search for someone young who could be trusted to tell him all that happened, and also look after the administration of what was left of the orphanage, ended when Mohan passed his school examinations.

Mohan met Narayanappa's requirements in several

ways. As he was a boy just out of school, Narayanappa's son was unlikely to feel threatened by his entry into the orphanage. He was also intelligent, loyal and knew enough arithmetic to provide Narayanappa a clear account of the current state of the sparse finances of the orphanage along with daily reports of the activities on the premises. Not that these reports made much of a difference. Narayanappa clearly did not have the will to pull up his son. A few half-hearted words of advice that he did manage on one of his son's visits home to collect money were quietly ignored.

After a while Narayanappa even lost interest in listening to Mohan's daily reports. As he couldn't conceivably sack him, having proclaimed himself the benefactor of Narasimhapura's most educated son, the task of listening to Mohan's daily reports fell to Narayanappa's grandson, Krishnappa, who had grown into quite a well-built young man. Krishnappa's opinion of his father had already been crystallised by his mother's strong views on the matter. All that Mohan told him about the orphanage only confirmed what he already knew. If he did not get bored with the daily visits it was only because he and Mohan had known each other quite well before Krishnappa had dropped out of school when his third attempt to clear class VII had failed.

On the face of it, Mohan and Krishnappa had very little in common. Mohan was the bright, hard-working favourite of the teachers. By the time he reached high school he was a fair, tall and handsome young man, always neatly dressed in clothes that were washed clean, if not always ironed. His hair was always well-oiled and combed and he never raised his voice. Krishnappa, on the other hand, wore bright-coloured clothes and never buttoned the top half of his shirt. He was as tall as Mohan but very much stouter. He was the only one in school whose voice was louder than that of the PT teacher. He enjoyed being rude, especially when there were girls around. If I am ever asked to pick two people completely different from each other, I will not look beyond Krishnappa and Mohan.

And yet they always seemed to complement each other. When they were classmates in a junior class in school, before Krishnappa began to fail with increasing regularity, it was Mohan who had helped him leave the house whenever he wanted, without permission. Krishnappa's method was a simple one. The toilet in his grandfather's house was some distance from the main house. Since the latch to the toilet door was broken, whoever used the toilet would leave some part of their daily wear outside as an indication that the toilet was in use. The older members of the family would leave their slippers, while young Krishnappa would leave his half pants. Krishnappa soon realised that if he disappeared after leaving his half pants outside the toilet door, his family would believe that he was in the toilet. Since Krishnappa came from a family where his roaming around without pants would be noticed even when he was very young, he needed a friend who would bring him another set of pants whenever he needed them. The friend had to be reliable, loyal and intelligent enough not to get caught. Mohan met all those conditions. And the friendship that began over having the right pants at the right place at the right time, grew over the years. In their adolescent years when Mohan was expected to present his daily reports on the orphanage to Krishnappa they inevitably spent more time covering a much wider range of topics from women to the latest movies and finally, to ways of making money.

It was on the last topic that Krishnappa found Mohan's

views most interesting. It was Mohan who pointed out the wastage involved in Narayanappa's tractor being used only to plough his fields in a nearby village, when it could be used very profitably to bring people in the evening from the village to see the films at Narasimhapura's Lakshmi Talkies. A couple of years later when the success of his tractor service to Lakshmi Talkies had prompted Krishnappa to consider buying a second tractor, it was Mohan who pointed out that it would be much more profitable to buy a second-hand van for this purpose. It was Mohan again who convinced Krishnappa not to name the van 'Sholay Transports' as a tribute to the latter's favourite Hindi movie. As Mohan had predicted, the name 'Sri Rama Transports' convinced Krishnappa's mother that her son would not go his father's way. As Sri Rama Transports grew to become the largest transport network not just in Narasimhapura but in the entire district, all major decisions were invariably taken on Mohan's advice. It was Mohan who thought up the idea of selling season tickets at the main office, so that the conductors could not benefit from carrying passengers at half the regular fare. It was Mohan who had suggested keeping the local police on their payroll instead of bribing them only when the buses were stopped for being overloaded. As a result Sri Rama Transports could carry out more trips with overloaded buses, while its competitors were stopped even when their buses were barely full.

It was Mohan again who had raised the possibility of Krishnappa using his growing transport network to revive his grandfather's political contacts. When political workers from Narayanappa's party had come to hire some buses to take people from the villages around Narasimhapura for a massive political rally in Bangalore, Krishnappa had argued over the price, even wanting double his normal rates. But Mohan had called him aside and asked him to provide the buses free of cost, promising that later benefits would far outweigh the immediate gains of charging a higher rate. Krishnappa had not understood what Mohan meant, but had by then learnt to trust the judgement of someone whose business sense he did not question.

Later, Krishnappa realised the wisdom of filling his buses with people who would, in return for a day's excursion to Bangalore, shout slogans in his favour. By the time of the fourth rally people in Bangalore began to recognise Krishnappa, and ministers even acknowledged his subservient greetings. He then began to request politicians in Bangalore to alter postings of officials stationed in Narasimhapura. He was not always successful, but those who did not want to be transferred out of Narasimhapura were wary of his much touted clout in Bangalore. The local police constable, who had a mistress in Narasimhapura, as well as the tahsildar, who owned land in a nearby village, no longer needed to be bribed to follow Krishnappa's orders.

The clout everyone thought Krishnappa had in Bangalore had its unpredictable consequences too. The sub-inspector, Nanjappa, the one who had paid a bribe for a more lucrative posting, made it a point to provoke Krishnappa in the hope of being transferred out of Narasimhapura. But these were minor irritants in Krishnappa's smooth progress in politics, from being the grandson of a respected but impoverished local politician to becoming a politician in his own right with an independent source of finance.

▲▼

You can now very well understand my surprise on hearing

about any connection between Mohan and Savitri. Mohan was the right-hand man of Narasimhapura's main politician; the man who represented all the old families of Narasimhapura as well as most of its older business interests and whose mother had, prompted by her unfortunate personal experience, begun Narasimhapura's anti-arrack movement. Savitri, on the other hand, was new to Narasimhapura; she had started a parallel anti-arrack movement which gained prominence when Krishnappa's grandfather had aged and when his mother had insisted that the women in the movement trust her son as much as she did. And, perhaps worst of all, Savitri had the support of the younger generation of Barkis who were quick to take the side of any movement which would help them dissociate themselves from their modest beginnings in Narasimhapura selling vade outside arrack shops.

It was obvious that Rajalakshmi's suspicions were, as usual, without any basis, but it was still a bit of a surprise because even she should have had more sense than to connect two people so clearly on opposite sides of the fence. While I normally would have listened to her story without pointing out the obvious signs of paranoia, I felt that this time she had gone too far. If she repeated this story to others less concerned about her welfare than me she could well get a violent response, especially from one of the Barki boys or from those muscular 'students' of the Government High School who hung around Krishnappa. So I told her, as gently as I could, that she was clearly mistaken; while it was always good to keep track of what one's husband was doing she couldn't expect people to believe such outrageous stories, and if she could tell me where she got the story from I would point out her obvious misunderstanding of the situation. It was then that she dropped the bombshell.

'Mohan told me,' she said. 'Last night when he came home late he said he had a fight with Krishnappa. I was naturally surprised and asked him why. And he was quite willing to tell me. He said it was because he had met Savitri when Krishnappa had told him not to.'

I couldn't quite follow her and told her so.

'I don't see what you can't follow. Mohan met Savitri and Krishnappa did not approve. Mohan himself told me so. He did not even have the decency to hide the fact that he was seeing that slut. In fact, he seemed to want to tell the whole world about it. He even told me that I should tell you.'

'Tell me what?' I asked, my surprise rapidly becoming consternation.

'Aren't you listening to anything I am saying! He specifically told me to tell you that he had broken up with Krishnappa because of that slut. He kept repeating it. Even this morning he asked me not to forget to tell you.'

This seemed quite serious. I just couldn't believe it. I kept wondering what could be the cause of this sudden split between Mohan and Krishnappa. Liking Savitri was one thing. Everyone liked the looks of that girl. I have admitted it to you myself. But if everyone started breaking off all established relationships just because of little girls, what would happen to the world? Being a well-read man, I know girls have had that effect on people. There was that fellow in England, or somewhere, who had given up his throne to marry a common woman. But such things only happened abroad. They did not happen in India, or at least not in Narasimhapura.

Rajalakshmi's story had shaken me so much that I kept brooding for a long time. When I finally looked at my watch it was half past one. It was only then that it struck me that Gopalakrishna had not made his usual visit to the office at noon. This had me puzzled. While it no doubt meant that the family intended giving me complete control over the paper, I had not expected him to withdraw so completely, so soon. I did not want it to look as if I had lost all respect for Bhimanna's family barely two days after his passing away. I decided to visit Bhimanna's house that evening, on the pretext of asking Gopalakrishna for instructions. He would then be able to make it clear that I was on my own, and that I could run the paper as I thought fit.

When I left the office to have my usual lunch-time dosa and coffee at Sri Venkateswara Cafe I was in a much more sombre mood than I had been in the morning. As I was walking down the wooden stairs, I was almost pushed aside by Puttaswamy who was charging up, his long legs taking the steps two at a time.

'What is your hurry?' I snapped at him.

'I am sorry, I am sorry, I am sorry,' he panted.

'It's okay. But what is your hurry anyway?'

'It's so tense outside. I hope Sati's peace meeting today will help calm the tensions.'

I didn't see why tension on the streets should make anyone charge up the stairs. But I didn't tell him so. The boy was bound to be feeling guilty considering it was his story that had created all the tension. So I put my arm around him to comfort him.

'You shouldn't take it personally,' I told him. 'Everyone makes mistakes. You may have written the story without any idea of what the consequences could be. You are still a young man. When you have my experience you will be able to judge such situations in your sleep.'

I would have thought words like those would have comforted the young man. After all how many senior journalists would have taken so much care to help him forget his blunder? But I was mistaken.

'What do you mean by 'my mistakes'!' he shouted. 'I did not commit any mistakes. I gave you a well-reasoned and balanced copy. It was you who distorted it. It was you who ruined my reputation as a journalist. If there is tension on the streets it is entirely your fault. If any blood flows from clashes between the Old Residents and the Barkis it will be on your conscience.'

My sympathy was clearly wasted on this young scoundrel. This has happened to me so often in the past. Just when you go out of your way to help someone, he turns around and snaps at you. I looked up at Rajalakshmi who had come to the top of the stairs to find out who Puttaswamy was screaming at. And she was suitably astonished to find that I was his target.

'You ask her,' I said nodding to Rajalakshmi, 'whose fault it is. Was it my story or yours that started this tension?'

'How can you blame Sir?' Rajalakshmi asked Puttaswamy with every bit of the devotion towards me that I expected from her. 'Where would you be without him? You have just started in the profession and you already think you know more than him?'

'It's all right, Rajalakshmi,' I said, introducing as deep a sense of hurt into my tone as I possibly could. 'As the Bhagwad Gita says, when you do good for people you must not expect anything in return.'

I then told Puttaswamy sternly, as I began walking down the stairs, 'I will personally cover the peace meeting this afternoon. It will give you a chance to see how sensitive meetings are covered.'

▲ **4** ▼

Over dosa and coffee at the old tea-shop that had now been expanded into a restaurant called Sri Venkateswara Cafe, my thoughts went back to more important issues that Puttaswamy always managed to divert my mind from. As I went past the counter to my usual place at the granite-topped table near the window, I told myself I had to be sure that when I met Gopalakrishna I would say nothing that would force him to act rashly and decide to run the paper himself. By the time I had settled into the formica-laminated chair and given my order to the waiter whose dhoti was folded up well above his knees, I had decided that it was perhaps better that I did not show too great an interest in the paper. When the waiter, who had relayed my order to the kitchen at the top of his voice, came back a little later with my dosa dripping with oil, I was convinced that it was a good thing I had decided to cover the peace meeting myself. It would ensure that I did not reach Bhimanna's house too early.

I then finished my dosa and coffee in so leisurely a manner that it would normally have led to a long queue of customers waiting for my chair. But the tension in the town had reduced the lunch hour rush. After paying my bill at the counter near the door, I walked slowly towards the place of the peace meeting. As I strolled down the less busy part of Mahatma Gandhi Road, oblivious of the sun, I couldn't help admiring the political sense of that girl, Savitri, which made her choose Barkisthal as the venue for the meeting. This place was sacred to her main supporters, the Barkis. As the story goes, the earliest Barkis decided to stop over at Narasimhapura when the bullock cart in which the leader of that caravan was travelling broke down while crossing a grazing ground near the town. The Barkis had set up camp near the broken down bullock cart and trekked to Narasimhapura every day. Later, when they had gained an economic foothold in Narasimhapura, they began to live within the town, but they retained an attachment for the place where the bullock cart had broken down. They would hold community meetings there, and the mass feeding after the death of any leading member of the Barki community was always held at Barkisthal, as it was called. Since it was on the other side of the town from the highway it attracted few passers-by, and was not in that sense a very good place for political meetings.

But what made the choice of Barkisthal politically astute was the old bullock cart. Some twenty years ago, when Bhimanna had raised enough resources to extend his business interests from arrack to the local hotel, he felt it necessary to make some sort of a gesture to the Barkis who had done so much to make his arrack business successful. He offered to build a monument to the old bullock cart. A large concrete platform was built and the remains of the bullock cart were placed on it. *The Narasimhapura Post* was given the task of making the inauguration of the monument a major event. This was done very well, even if I say so myself, by presenting the monument as a symbol of unity between the Old Residents and the Barkis. The monument was named Res-Barki and it occupied the centre of the large open area that was Barkisthal. As part of our efforts to promote the Res-Barki the whole of Barkisthal was beautified. It was surrounded by a ring of coconut trees and the green grass that was planted in Barkisthal made it stand out against the dry land around it. What better place could there have been for a rally for amity between the Barkis and the Old Residents?

As I turned left at the end of Mahatma Gandhi Road I could see Barkisthal across the open fields. Even from a distance I could see that this would not be one of Savitri's usual meetings. Whenever she called a dharna in front of our office, or even when she led one of her morchas, she normally needed to make up with noise what she lacked in numbers. Her 'mass mobilisations' usually consisted of a small group of young women, surrounded by the young men that such a group would naturally attract.

But the crowd today was very much larger. I couldn't help admiring her political determination as I realised she had reached out to more sections of Narasimhapura's population than she ever had before. Having mobilised people on this scale she could no longer be dismissed as a novice in Narasimhapura's political scene. But as I moved closer to Barkisthal something told me that everything was not all right. As I looked at some of the people in the crowd I couldn't help wondering whether they were really there to express their support for Savitri. As I had expected, Puttaswamy was there right in front though he did not have to cover the meeting, just to show that he was more interested in peace than anyone else. Mohan's presence in the same row too would have surprised me more if I had not heard Rajalakshmi's tale. But it was the crowd at the back that had me really worried. It extended right upto the semicircular stone boundary wall of Barkisthal, which being low and quite broad has always been used as a bench by vistors. One end of this wall was occupied by the Barki boys, which was only to be expected. It was the occupants of the wall on the other side that worried me. Seated here were a large number of boys from Government High School who were believed to be close to Krishnappa. And standing around them were all the muscular drivers and cleaners of Krishnappa's transport network. Surely, they couldn't have put their jobs at risk by being present at the political rally called by someone their employer strongly disliked?

What made me really apprehensive was the sight of Kittiappa standing on the wall, twirling his moustache. Kittiappa was Krishnappa's hatchet man, and looked every bit his role. His short stocky frame was wrapped in a dhoti that must have once been white. His bloodshot eyes sunk deep into his dark face gave him a fierce look, which his huge moustache, twirled into sharp points on either side, only enhanced. He came from one of the larger landholding families in a village just beyond Barkisthal. He was barely out of his teens when he forced his father, at knife-point, to divide the family property. He ran through his share of the property quickly enough. He then claimed to be a tenant on his uncle's land. A combination of Krishnappa's political clout and the fear of Kittiappa's knife had seen the land tribunal awarding the land to Kittiappa. With him present, Savitri had to be very careful indeed.

She didn't seem to care, or was perhaps oblivious to the potential danger in the situation when she stood on top of the Res-Barki platform and began to speak. I was just a bit surprised that she chose to speak in the local language. As I expected, her Kannada was halting and heavily accented. And she tried to make up for it by adopting the form of address favoured by local politicians.

'Mothers and fathers, brothers and sisters and friends, I am talking to you here today at a time of great distress to all of us. The old amity between different groups in Narasimhapura, the amity that was the main feature of this town, the amity that Narasimhapura was proud of, has now been threatened. There are more policemen today in Narasimhapura than there have ever been before. The tension that is in the air today is something that our mothers and fathers had never known. Even at the time of the partition of this great country, Narasimhapura had been an oasis of peace. But today the liquor barons and politicians have joined together to break this tradition of peace.'

I couldn't help smiling at the thought that Savitri believed that what had been written in *The Narasimhapura Post* was connected to Bhimanna's liquor business. But others were not going to take it as lightly. A voice from the back shouted 'Don't speak ill of the dead.' But Savitri continued as if she had not heard.

'There comes a time in the history of a city when vested interests set out to destroy it in the pursuit of their own vulgar dreams. In their pursuit of short-term consumerist goals they do not care if they destroy the future. They may be willing to destroy the future of their children, but we cannot let them destroy our future, the future of our children. We must fight for our rights, we must fight for peace. We cannot let these vested interests rule over us. We must be willing to sacrifice our lives for this cause. I am willing to give every drop of my blood to see that the peaceful character of Narasimhapura is not disturbed. We must stand together and arm ourselves at least with lathis so that we are ready to fight groups that try to disturb the peace. They must be made to realise that any effort to break the peace will not go unchallenged! Our blood will flow on the streets of Narasimhapura before they have their way!'

An old lady sitting in front spoke up softly. 'Why do you keep talking of blood, amma? If we want peace let us talk softly. Why do you want to speak in a way that only angers other people?'

The lady's softly spoken comment struck a chord with those who could hear her. A young man in the front row stood up and suggested that no angry speeches should be made, and that everyone should disperse after standing in silence for two minutes.

But Savitri was quick to pounce on him.

'Do you see this?' she asked the audience. 'We have hardly begun and this young man wants to surrender. He thinks we should sit silently and let others break the amity that Narasimhapura is famous for. It was this kind of weakness that allowed Hitler to gain support in Germany. Fascist forces always thrive on the weakness of the forces opposing them. Are we cowards? Must we die like sheep without a fight?'

There was a loud roar of 'No' from a section of the crowd. I couldn't help noticing that this support was loudest from the corner where the Barki boys had gathered.

I glanced nervously at the other corner where the Government High School boys were crowded together with Krishnappa's drivers and cleaners. There had been an angry murmur from them when Savitri had mentioned local politicians being behind the tension, and now they were visibly restless.

But Savitri kept looking only at the section of the crowd that was cheering her, and her tone took on an even higher pitch. 'Let us see who will be able to stop us from keeping peace in Narasimhapura. Let some politicians not think that by merely hiring a few goondas they will be able to destroy the will of the people of Narasimhapura. Beginning today we will place a rose on the Res-Barki every day as a symbol of Narasimhapura's unity. We will create a group of armed young men who will fight any effort to destroy peace by goondas hired by local politicians.'

The repeated references to Krishnappa were too much for his followers to take. Shouts of 'Savitri Murdabad!' rent the air. As her followers countered with shouts of 'Savitri Zindabad!', the older people started leaving. Anyone could see that the meeting was heading towards a violent clash. I also moved towards the edge of the crowd and stepped over the low bench-wall of Barkisthal so that I could make a quick dash to safety even while trying to follow as much of the proceedings as I could.

Savitri was now making an effort to control her supporters. 'Please stay calm. They have been sent here to provoke us. We must not attack them. If they were a civilised group I would have invited them to a debate on this issue. Even now I challenge any of them to come to the platform and debate the issue. See, none of them is willing to debate the issue.'

But Savitri had spoken too soon. To her surprise, and mine as well, the Government High School boys started shouting that they were willing to debate the issue. And they chose, of all people, Kittiappa to put forward their case.

Kittiappa leapt down from the wall, ran up to the platform and jumped on to it with such speed that even Savitri took an involuntary step back. He stood for a few minutes on top of the platform waving out to his supporters with one hand and twirling his moustache with the other. After a couple of minutes of waving with his right hand he began to wave with his left hand while twirling his moustache with his right. After a few more minutes of this he took the green towel that was slung across his shoulder and tied it into a turban around his head. He then proceeded to wave again. Just when he had kept waving long enough for me to begin feeling he would step down from the platform without saying anything, he spoke the four words that were to shake Narasimhapura.

'We will break its,' he said.

At first nobody quite knew what he was talking about. His supporters did roar in appreciation, but that was only because he had said something just when they were about to give up hope of him uttering any word at all. And, as if to score a point over Savitri, he had said it in English. The sound of the applause prompted Kittiappa to repeat the four words in a sort of chant. 'We will break its, we will break its, we will break its.' That he followed the old Narasimhapura habit of using the plural even when it was incorrect added to the confusion. It was only after the initial applause had died down that Kittiappa made himself clear.

'We will break down the Res-Barki,' he declared.

This time his matter-of-fact statement was received with a hushed silence. Both sides suddenly realised the enormity of what had been said. The Res-Barki was not just a monument for the Barkis. It was very much a part of life for everyone in Narasimhapura. The Old Residents visited it almost as often as the Barkis did. It was the place old men regularly went to during their evening walks. On any day when it was not raining it was common to see groups of old men, both Old Residents and Barkis, sitting around discussing the politics of the country. Their presence gave the park the right atmosphere for young girls to come and chat. The presence of young girls made a daily visit to the Res-Barki a must for Narasimhapura's adolescent boys. And the presence of a lot of young men and women made it the natural place for newly-weds to come for a stroll in the first month of their marriage. Breaking down the Res-Barki was too shocking a threat, and it left the audience stunned into silence.

The first to react was Savitri. She ran in front of the Res-Barki and spread her arms wide. 'I will protect this with my life,' she said, switching back to English in her excitement.

Puttaswamy then jumped on to the platform and stood between Savitri and Kittiappa.

I do not know what it was about the two of them standing there facing Kittiappa that affected the audience. It may have been that most of Krishnappa's men thought Kittiappa had gone too far. Or it may have been the fact that the two of them made a rather striking picture. Even in the tension of the moment I couldn't help recognising the beauty of the scene: a tall, lanky Puttaswamy standing with his arms outstretched in front of a diminutive Savitri similarly poised against the backdrop of the evening sun. Or it may have been the fact that Savitri's pallav, which till that moment had been demurely draped around her shoulder, had fallen to the ground as a result of her dramatic gesture. Whatever the reason, frayed tempers were beginning to be soothed. One of the quieter Government High School boys, Thimanna, who was expected to break Narasimhapura's record for high school marks that Mohan had set long ago, walked up to the dais. He spoke to Kittiappa and in a few moments, I was sure, the meeting would have ended calmly.

But Savitri would have none of that. 'Let us finish the debate,' she screamed. 'You people are incapable of any argument. All you know is to shout.'

This time even the usually quiet Thimanna had gone red in the face, his large eyes opening really wide. 'Of course, we have far better arguments than you have,' Thimanna shouted back. 'It is just that you don't want to hear them.'

'And just what are the arguments for breaking so respected a monument as the Res-Barki?' Savitri asked, with the air of one who does not expect an answer.

But Thimanna was not one to give up so easily. Losing an argument to Savitri on a public platform was not just a matter of personal shame for him. As he saw it, it would mean he had let down all the Old Residents of Narasimhapura. He just had to find a reason to defend Kittiappa's rash statement. 'It has to be broken down because it hurts the pride of the Old Residents of Narasimhapura.'

He had me a bit surprised there. The Res-Barki was built by one of the more respected old families in Narasimhapura. And the general impression, created with not a little help from *The Narasimhapura Post*, was that it was more a tribute to the Old Residents than the Barkis. Savitri was quick to point this out in her more-forceful-than-necessary manner. This time I was among those who did not expect a reply from Thimanna.

But we had underestimated the boy.

'It has nothing to do with who built the Res-Barki.'

'Why not?' snapped Savitri.

'Because there are more important things than who built it.'

'Tell me one thing that is more important,' Savitri insisted.

Thimanna was nonplussed. His eyes grew so large that his eyelashes merged with his eyebrows. He was desperately trying to think of something about the monument that would be more important than the role of Bhimanna and other Old Residents in building it. And Savitri wasn't about to give him time to think.

'Tell me one thing that is more important,' she repeated.

As Thimanna just kept staring at her, she turned to the audience and announced with a triumphant smile: 'They don't have a reason!'

The loud cheer she got from the Barkis in response to her announcement was too much for Thimanna.

'That is not true!'

'Then tell me the reason,' Savitri demanded with the air of a headmistress asking a primary school student why he was late. Thimanna now just had to come up with an answer.

'That,' he said, pointing in the general direction of the Res-Barki.

'What?' asked Savitri.

'That,' Thimanna repeated with a gesture that was even more vague than the earlier one.

'See,' said Savitri with a smirk as she turned to address the audience, 'he simply keeps repeating 'that' as if he were a parrot. Let alone a reason, he cannot come up with more than a word.'

'That is because you cannot understand what I am saying!'

Savitri put her hands up to quieten her supporters.

'Let us try to understand the sophisticated argument that he is trying to develop,' she said, making no attempt to hide her condescension.

'That...that,' Thimanna started again.

I was now beginning to feel sorry for the boy. He looked quite puny standing next to Kittiappa and Puttaswamy. He was taller than Savitri, but not by much. And his stammering made him look even more pathetic.

But I needn't have worried. When he repeated 'that' a third time, it was different. He said it with so much confidence that even Savitri was taken aback. And the fact that he was pointing to the foundation of the Res-Barki gave his last 'that' a new meaning. Everyone was now craning their necks to try and see what he was pointing at. The resultant commotion gave him just the time he needed to compose his thoughts. When he spoke again it was with the finality of someone who has no doubt about what he had to say.

'Look at the stones that have been used in the foundation. Those stones were taken from the rock on which Narasimhapura's diety was found.'

This was a new one. Everyone in Narasimhapura knew

the legend that the idol of the goddess around which the town's main temple was built had been found in a field near Narasimhapura. But no one had, in the past, tried to identify the specific rock on which it had been found, let alone trace pieces of that rock to individual foundation stones.

But Thimanna's statement was just the tonic that Krishnappa's men needed, waiting as they were to counter Savitri's aggressiveness with aggressiveness of their own. Kittiappa made an angry speech, in Kannada, to the effect that the Barkis were trying to destroy the local deity. As the tension in the atmosphere rose, I quietly slipped out. And as I walked away I realised I had not left a moment too soon. The armed policemen who had waited patiently the whole afternoon were getting out of their vans, and moving quickly towards the Res-Barki.

▲▼

Once I reached Mahatma Gandhi Road I slowed down. I was quite far away from the crowd, I was out of breath and, in any case, I needed some time to gather my thoughts after the excitement of the afternoon. It was very important that I said the right things, and nothing but the right things, at Bhimanna's place. I had to be sure that I did not give the impression of being too eager to take over the paper, while at the same time I could not be too disinterested either. I also had to work out my version of what went wrong with *The Narasimhapura Post* the day Bhimanna died; a version that had to be clear enough to make an old lady realise the fault lay with her son, but not so clear as to force a mother to defend her son.

By the time I had strolled down the entire length of Mahatma Gandhi Road, turned on the highway and passed through the high steel-sheet gates of Bhimanna's house I was quite nervous. I had walked down that path to the main door many times before, but rarely had so much depended on what happened when I was at the house. As soon as I stepped inside, I went up to the old lady who was sitting on the floor in a corner of the large room behind the verandah. The maroon colour of one wall and the bottle green on the other made the corner very dark. I could not make out the expression on her face. But I was taking no chances.

I stood with my head appropriately bowed and began, 'I had been wanting to come and personally apologise for what happened to the paper the day he died. I will never be able to forgive myself. Rarely have we made such a major blunder. And that it should happen on the day he died is too much for me to take. I haven't been able to sleep thinking about the paper. And to think that I had planned it all in such great detail. I had even picked a photo of him that he used to always tell me you had liked. It was that old photo of him sitting on his 350cc motorcycle. He would have looked like a hero within the thick black border that I had planned. But look what happened. I had just sat down to...'

'I know,' she said.

I had expected this. I knew Gopalakrishna would have given her some distorted version of the story, and was quite prepared.

'Amma, I know you would have heard the story. But after all these years of service all I ask of you is one favour. Please allow me to present my side of the story. You have been more than a mother to me. I would gladly have given my life for Anna and you. All I ask is one chance to explain. After that if you want to cut my head off, I will die happy.'

'There is no need,' she said.

'But Amma, all I ask is one chance to explain how...'

'There is no need,' she repeated, 'because Gopalakrishna has told me it was not your fault. And that he was entirely to blame.'

This took me completely by surprise. I had never expected Gopalakrishna to be so generous. I suppose I had underestimated the boy. And when he entered the room I was feeling very warm towards him.

'I came here to pay my respects to your mother,' I told him. 'We were also wondering in the office why you had missed your regular visit at noon. We were very worried and hope nothing has gone wrong.'

'No, no, nothing at all,' Gopalakrishna said. 'It is just that I will not be coming to the office anymore.'

Just like that. All that I had expected was coming through very much more easily than I had ever dared to hope.

'But why?' I asked with all the concern I could muster at such short notice. 'I hope we have not done anything to upset you.'

'No, not at all. It is just that I have decided that I will not have anything further to do with the paper.'

'But surely,' I said, barely able to conceal my glee, 'you will visit us at least now and then.'

'I don't think so. I have decided to move back to Bombay. I have also convinced Amma that she should come to Bombay. After all, now that Anna is no more, she has no reason to stay here alone.'

This was turning out to be far better than I had

expected even in my wildest dreams. I had never thought that I would be in charge of *The Narasimhapura Post* with the owner hundreds of miles away.

'We will all be very sorry to see you go. We cannot think of *The Narasimhapura Post* without anyone from Bhimanna's family looking after it.'

And then he dropped the bombshell.

'Yes, I agree. *The Narasimhapura Post* is too closely associated with the family for it to be run when we are not there. That is why I have decided to close it down.'

'But, but, but,' I said, finding it difficult to move beyond that first word.

'But you can't,' I said, when I finally managed to do so.

'Why not?' he asked, as if he was genuinely curious.

'Because, I mean because, I mean…'

I don't know how many times I said 'because'. The fact is I just could not think of a good reason why the family should not close down a loss-making paper when they were breaking all ties with Narasimhapura. Of course, there were a lot of good reasons, like my career, poor Rajalakshmi being without a job; but these were our reasons, not Gopalakrishna's. Then out of sheer desperation I blurted out: 'But you don't have to close it down, you can sell it.'

'Sell it? Who will want to buy this loss-making paper. I have always wondered why Anna didn't close it down much earlier.'

'It is because it is influential.' I did not like his smile when I said that, but I carried on nevertheless, 'It influences a lot of people in Narasimhapura.'

'Like who?'

I couldn't at that moment think of a single bloody name.

'Okay,' he said, 'I am quite willing to sell it. But a buyer must be found before my mother and I leave Narasimhapura next week.'

Next week, I thought as I walked out. Was that all the time I had? After all these years, was my future to be decided in just one week?

The same thoughts kept going around in my mind. I just couldn't think of anything else. I was well into Mahatma Gandhi Road, well past Jai Hind Novelty Stores, when I noticed that something was wrong. There was nobody on the road. I had barely realised this when a lathi was thrown at me, bouncing just a couple of feet away. As I looked up, the owner of the lathi, in his policeman's uniform, was running up to me.

'Get off the street,' he said. 'Don't you know there is a curfew?'

'A curfew?' I couldn't help asking. 'But why?'

'Because there was police firing at the Barkisthal and two of the Barkis were killed. Now get off the street before I arrest you.'

I ran to the office, as I was still too far away from home. All I could think of was: perhaps it would have been better if I had just stayed at the Barkisthal and got shot. At least it would have been a quick death and I wouldn't have had to bother about the one week Gopalakrishna had given me.

As I entered the office I could hear the pounding of typewriter keys. Even before I saw him I could make out from the racket that it was Puttaswamy. In more normal circumstances I would have given him a lecture on how to use the typewriter properly rather than attack it with two fingers. But I was too tired for that.

As soon as he saw me enter, he stood up.

'About the story, sir,' he began.

I was about to ask him what story he was talking about when I remembered I had told him I would cover the afternoon's peace meeting. The events of the afternoon and evening had made me completely forget about it. I was not in the mood to sit down and write out some rubbish.

'Why don't you write it out? You were there, weren't you?'

His face lit up. You would have thought I had asked him to cover the Olympics. Since he was in such an enthusiastic mood, I thought I might as well make the best of it.

'Why don't you also check everything else? You know, the proofs, the printer and everything.'

His response was once again so gleeful that I should perhaps have been suspicious. But I was far too tired, both physically and mentally, to care. In any case the paper was going to close down. I went into Bhimanna's room and sat down on the chair only he had ever sat on, and stared at the table with its green baize tablecloth. At least that hadn't changed. The table and its tablecloth still looked as overwhelming as they did on the day I had first joined *The Narasimhapura Post*. The sense of adventure that I felt when I used to sneak into the room at night to sleep on the table was no longer there. But the sight of the table with its serene tablecloth, as always, took my mind back to where it had all begun. As the old memories returned, so did an inexplicable desire to sleep on the table again. I now needed to curl up to be able to sleep on it, but I did want to try. I walked over to the door and closed it, without bothering to slip the latch. And when I lay down on the table I fell asleep almost immediately. The warmth of the old memories and the tablecloth helped me sleep more comfortably than I had for years.

▲ 5 ▼

It was well past nine the next morning when I woke up. I would perhaps have slept even longer, if I had not felt something poking into my stomach. At first I thought it was my acidity playing up again. All the excitement of the last couple of days was bound to hurt sooner or later. After a few seconds I felt the sharp pain again. This time it distinctly felt as if a stick was being poked into my stomach. I opened my eyes to find myself staring at the ugly face of Nanjappa. I immediately closed my eyes tight and turned so that I faced the other side. I remained curled up on the desk, hugging my knees even tighter. This had to be a nightmare, I told myself. The last two days had been bad enough when I had got up on the right side of the bed and seen the Lord's face first thing in the morning. I couldn't bear to think what the day would be like after seeing Nanjappa's face before anything else. This just had to be a nightmare.

But there was no such luck. A firm stab on my spine

with his stick made sure that I was not only awake but off the table, clutching my back.

'What do you want?' I rasped, not having had the time to force myself to adopt the subservient tone that I normally used with Nanjappa.

'Don't you dare talk to me like that,' he said sharply. 'Who the hell do you think you are? You should thank your stars I didn't break your spine. I have a good mind to do so now. You have been doing nothing but creating trouble in this bloody town. It is bad enough having to work here when things are quiet. But with you going around provoking everybody to kill each other, I have not been able to go home early the last two nights. I thought I had warned you yesterday morning. But today again you have used that damn rag to create tension. If you think you can get away with it you are mistaken. I have come to arrest you. And let me tell you nobody in the government is going to help you. None of them wants a riot so close to elections. Once I can show them that you are a troublemaker, they will look the other way even if your body stinks after I have finished with you.'

Oh my God, I thought. This *had* to be a nightmare. I didn't have a clue as to what he was talking about. I had not done a thing in the paper since yesterday. But I knew enough about Nanjappa's methods to realise that the problem was what he would do and not what I had or had not done. Everyone knew that one of the reasons he was posted to Narasimhapura from Bangalore was because of the methods he had used in a police station against a student who was on his annual agitation. The way he was looking at me now with that little smirk on his face as he kept tapping his stick into the palm of his left hand sent a chill down my spine. My knees felt weak and I dropped to the floor.

Fortunately for me Nanjappa thought that I was falling on my knees to touch his feet. He moved one foot forward helpfully and I grabbed it as soon as I realised that it might just mollify him. I looked up at his face and pleaded with tears in my eyes.

'You must save me,' I said. 'You have been a protector of Narasimhapura and everyone here. I have always told everybody that our very existence here depends on your protection. I do not know what I have done to deserve your anger. But whatever it is I will take any punishment you decide. All I ask is that you believe me when I tell you that I don't know what I have done wrong.'

'Do you take me for a fool?' he asked, but his tone was a little softer. 'Your whole paper is full of it and you tell me you don't know anything about it? The situation was bad enough last night after the show that slut put up against Krishnappa's men. But today after what you have published any hope we had of getting some kind of peace in the town has disappeared, and you dare to ask me what you have done?'

It was only then that I realised he was angry about something that had appeared in *The Narasimhapura Post*. Most people don't seem to realise that editors cannot always know what comes in their papers. I remember once when Puttaswamy had written something about what had happened in West Germany under Stallion or Lennon or someone else. Everybody wanted to know what had happened to me to allow such stories in *The Narasimhapura Post*. Nobody believed me when I told them that I had nothing to do with it, and that Puttaswamy had put in the article by himself. And what my own friends could not believe, I could hardly expect Nanjappa to accept.

'It is all journalism,' I said. 'We have to carry both sides of the story. We carried one side today, so in tomorrow's paper we will carry the other side. You will be surprised about how balanced you will find the paper. In all my years in journalism no one has told me that I was unbalanced. Sometimes we might tilt to one side, but we always make up by tilting to the other side the next time. Even a tightrope walker may tilt to one side on one day by mistake. But as long as he tilts to the other side immediately there is no problem.'

'I don't care which side you tilt,' Nanjappa said. 'Nobody will ask any questions if I arrest you now. But if you create some more trouble for me, everybody will jump on me for not arresting you.'

The words were worrying but there was something in the tone that gave me hope.

'If you arrest me I can do nothing to help improve things.'

'What can you do?'

'I could write pieces balancing what appeared today.' I knew it wasn't the best of responses but his reply made it look a lot worse.

'You could write those pieces from prison as well.'

'I have to ensure that nobody else writes anything that can disturb the peace.'

'You did not manage that yesterday. Or are you telling me that you are directly responsible for what has appeared in the paper today?'

'No, no, not at all,' I said. And in desperation I added, 'Actually there is a very different reason why I should stay out. But I do not know how to tell you. Bhimanna and I had been planning a welcome for you for quite some time. We thought we would have a large party with drinks and food and all the important people of Narasimhapura. But now that he is no more it wouldn't be right. It would not also be right for me to keep the money, especially since he wanted to spend a thousand rupees. I do not know if the money will remain safe in my house in my absence. I don't trust the little girl who comes to sweep the place. It would be much better if I gave it to you right away.'

I can't remember having packaged a bribe better than that. And I could see that the policeman in Nanjappa couldn't help appreciating the fact.

'I am not interested in such things,' he said. 'Even when ministers have wanted to give me presents I have not accepted. However, since you say it was Bhimanna who had suggested it, perhaps I should accept it so that his soul rests in peace.'

My relief must have been clear on my face, for he was quick to take on a firmer tone. 'But don't think that means you can get away with writing whatever you like. I will be seeing tomorrow's paper and if you have not brought back the balance, I will come to arrest you.'

▲▼

It was a while after he left that I managed to calm myself down. I then came out of Bhimanna's small office to the larger room and picked up a copy of the paper, so that I could at least know on which side I had to lean to get back the balance. And my first glance at the paper sent a chill down my spine.

The main headline ran across the eight columns of the paper screaming, 'Barkis to fight to the last drop of their blood'. Below it was a huge picture of Savitri, waving her finger at the gods. There were only two other stories on the page and neither headline was soothing. 'Krishnappa's men begin riot' was one. And next to it was a boxed item saying, of all things, that the Barkis were expecting reinforcements from home to help fight the Old Residents. My hands were trembling as I held the paper and attempted to read the lead story.

> On a day of dramatic developments the battle lines were drawn today between those seeking peace and the intolerant among the Old Residents. Our leader, Ms.Savitri Rao, firmly gave a call to stand up to the tyranny of the intolerant among the Old Residents. Despite grave risk to her life she fought to protect the Res-Barki which was under attack by goondas hired by Krishnappa. Ms.Rao said the Barkis had nothing to fear and that blood will flow like a river in every street in Narasimhapura if the Old Residents did not give up their attack on the Barkis. She said she would personally arm the Barkis if Krishnappa and his goondas did not back down and recognise that the Barkis were an integral part of Narasimhapura and had a greater right to lead Narasimhapura than corrupt Old Residents like Krishnappa.

I couldn't bring myself to read anymore. I turned the page to see if there was any more of this stuff and found that my worst fears had come true. There were direct attacks on Krishnappa in almost every story. There was even a virulent profile of him under the title, 'Is this man a politician or a scoundrel?' And the whole of the last page was covered with an article that appeared to be more sober, but was perhaps the most damaging of all. It was a huge piece by someone called Dr. Lakshmi Subbalakshmi which claimed there was historical evidence that the Barkis had, in fact, been residents of Narasimhapura a thousand years ago and had left the town due to a drought. The coming of the Barkis was thus only a homecoming, and if anyone had to leave Narasimhapura it was the Old Residents as the Barkis were actually older residents than the Old Residents. The article was accompanied by a picture of two tiny bits of paper that looked to me like worn-out postage stamps, but which the caption insisted were old Barki coins found near the Narasimhapura bus-stand.

My knees were wobbling as I put the paper down. When I had asked Puttaswamy to look after the edition last night I had known he would be biased in favour of Savitri, but I had not expected this. Surely even that stupid fellow would have known the damage that this edition could cause? Surely even he couldn't have been so stupid as to think that he could attack Krishnappa in Narasimhapura and get away with it? Surely even with his subhuman intelligence he could have seen that an article insisting that the Old Residents should be thrown out of Narasimhapura, so that the Barkis could live there, would cause the town to explode? The more I thought of it, the more I found it difficult to keep my temper under control. And when he entered the office five minutes later, whistling calmly, I had to restrain myself from wringing his neck.

'What the hell do you mean by this?' I asked, shaking the paper in front of his face. 'Who the hell gave you permission to bring out an edition like this?'

'You asked me to bring out the edition,' he said with irritating calmness. 'So I brought it out in a manner I thought fit.'

'You think it was right to bring out a rag like this? You

think you have the right to attack prominent citizens like Krishnappa, especially when he was nowhere near the scene. If at all anyone had to be attacked it was that bitch Savitri. She was the one who started it all.'

'Don't you dare call her such names,' he hissed. At least I had removed the supercilious smile from the young idiot's face.

'Why not?' I asked. 'You people say you are educated. You talk of values in journalism. And is this all you can do?'

'There is nothing in the paper that goes against my values in journalism, or her values in politics.'

'Nothing?' I rasped. I was losing what little control I had over myself. 'You don't find anything wrong in what you have done? What about this story which gives only her point of view? I was present and I know that other points of view were also mentioned.'

'I presented what I thought were the most important points of view. It goes against my principles to treat rabble-rousing Old Residents on par with secular leaders like Sati.'

'And I suppose it does not go against your principles to call Krishnappa a scoundrel, even though he was not present?'

'I have to write what I believe. And I can tell you in all honesty that I believe he is a scoundrel.'

'And this last page. Where did you get this rubbish from? Who is this great historian who has suddenly found out about the history of the Barkis?'

'I wrote that article,' he said without batting an eyelid.

'You wrote that article claiming to be an eminent historian?'

'Well, I was studying history and if I had not given up

my research because of my commitment to a small town newspaper I would have been an eminent historian.'

'It was not against your lofty principles to pretend that the author was a PhD?'

'What a fuss you are making about my using the 'Dr.' as a prefix. Nowadays PhD's are a dime a dozen. I just used it so that it sounded authentic. And in any case if the whole name is a pseudonym, so is the prefix.'

'And it didn't bother your great principles that this article has caused so much violence and cost human lives?'

'In a fight for a just cause it is only the weak who bother about human lives.'

'Really? Then why didn't you use your own name? Wasn't it because you were scared?'

'I do not believe the article would have had the same impact if I had used my own name. It would have seemed very subjective.'

'And I suppose it had nothing to do with you not wanting to be one among those poor bastards who are dying in this conflict?'

'That is the trouble with you old men,' he said with that supercilious smile of his. 'You do not realise the importance of tactics in political struggle. It should be obvious that it would not have benefited the struggle if I had sacrificed my life at this point.'

There was no point talking to the idiot. He had not only created this mess but had the audacity to be pompous about it. I had to think of ways of getting out of it. It was all very well to tell Nanjappa that I would balance the paper the next day, but this was not something I could do very easily. It was not as if my relationship with Krishnappa was so warm that I could go to him and expect him to present his case even after the vicious attack our paper had made on him that morning. In fact, if he had known that I was to be arrested for the coverage he would certainly have found a way to ensure that I did not escape. As everybody in Narasimhapura knew, Krishnappa and I did not even acknowledge each other's presence on the few occasions that we happened to be in the same place.

Looking back now, there was nothing in what had happened to make us enemies for life. It was a minor dispute about a housing society. Krishnappa had spotted some land on what was then the outskirts of Narasimhapura and had come to an arrangement with the owner to convert it into house sites. He was to use his political contacts to get permission to convert the agricultural land into urban land, and in return would get fifty per cent of the proceeds from the sale of the sites. Since Krishnappa had not invested any money, and I felt he might need some assistance to get the required permission, I had offered to help him in return for only a quarter of the proceeds from the sale of the sites. Though he had refused my kind offer in very rude terms, I had not said anything to him and would have been happy to remain a friend.

It just so happened that when the local member of parliament was in Narasimhapura I had mentioned to him the need for a journalists' colony in the town and pointed out that there was this owner of agricultural land who was running after Krishnappa to get it converted into urban land. I told the MP that if he allowed me to arrange for the conversion of the land it would help the cause of local journalism. He readily agreed and, after some delay, converted the land. The sites were then sold by the Narasimhapura Senior Journalists' Cooperative Society, with

The Last Post

half the returns being given to the original owner of the land and the other half being retained by the Society.

I learnt later that the delay had been because of Krishnappa objecting to the proposal. I believe he had gone to the minister and told him that I was the only genuine member of the cooperative and the other names were fictitious. As if the validity of a cooperative society was to be determined by the number of genuine members. Was it my fault that I was the only senior journalist in Narasimhapura who wanted a site at that time? Luckily the minister was a practical man and recognised that if people waited for the laws to be strictly followed, nothing would get done in the country. Despite his vicious actions I was still quite willing to maintain a friendly relationship with Krishnappa and even went to his house to shake hands and forget about the past. But he called me foul names and threw me out of his house. He was like that. He had no culture. I wonder what he would have done if he had been in America or England where people always shake hands after a good fight.

As if that wasn't bad enough Krishnappa had also complained to Bhimanna about my getting half the proceeds of the sites sold in the new colony. He had distorted the picture completely and made it look as if I was using my association with *The Narasimhapura Post* to get unfair advantage. He also told Bhimanna that if he wasn't careful I would end up taking over *The Narasimhapura Post*. Bhimanna wouldn't normally have listened to such rubbish, but Krishnappa must have caught him in a weak moment for I could spot a touch of suspicion when I met Bhimanna soon after the sale of the first site. Luckily for me I had anticipated that Krishnappa would do something like this and had decided to offer the proceeds from the first sale to Bhimanna as a mark of my respect for him. The moment I saw his mood I quickly raised the offer to the proceeds from the sale of the first five sites. This made him feel a lot better and I was also able to tell those who had lent Krishnappa their ears that I was not the only beneficiary of the earnings of the Senior Journalists' Society. Bhimanna had still been quite worried about the impact of Krishnappa's continuing hostility on *The Narasimhapura Post*. And it was on his suggestion that I decided to offer Rajalakshmi a job. As Mohan's wife she had access to the one man Krishnappa was then known to trust. Over the years, as I became the pillar she leant on, *The Narasimhapura Post* had all the access to Krishnappa that it needed.

That is, until the moment when we needed it the most. Just when access to Krishnappa had become imperative for my existence outside prison, that idiot Mohan had to break away from him all because of a silly girl. Not that it would have been easy to get Rajalakshmi to approach her husband, given the mood she was in. When she had walked into the office braving the very tense situation on the streets, I knew that she had come there only to get away from home. And as she kept staring at the typewriter with an intensity that could have bored holes into its metal frame, I knew it would be futile to get her to talk about anything other than Mohan and his affair. As if that was the only thing in the world. At a time when the whole future was at stake it was only Rajalakshmi who could have spent her time thinking about a relationship that had the least bearing on *The Narasimhapura Post*. It was quite ridiculous.

Or was it?

It suddenly struck me that thinking about that silly affair may not be all that ridiculous at a time like this. In fact, all things considered, it was probably the only thing *I* should have been thinking about. After all, what I needed was something to allow me direct access to Krishnappa. What could be better than pleading the case of his once-trusted lieutenant's wife? Rajalakshmi was clearly the aggrieved party. As she had no one else to go to, she would have to approach Krishnappa. Since she couldn't possibly go to his house alone, especially with all the tension in town, she needed to be accompanied by a man. Preferably an older man, a father figure, so that people did not get any funny ideas. And I was the only older man available. It was the perfect excuse to meet Krishnappa. And I could then also broach the topic of the riot. After all when the whole town was talking about it, it would be unusual if I didn't. The more I thought about it, the better it looked. Surely even that oaf couldn't throw me out when I was accompanying a lady in distress.

    I walked across to Rajalakshmi's table, barely managing to hide my excitement, and asked her, in keeping with our ritual, why she was gloomy. But instead of her usual it-is-all-my-karma outpour, she just stared at me. And after staring at me for what seemed eternity, she burst into tears.

    I was stumped. I just did not know what to do. This was quite embarrassing. Whenever she had cried in the office in the past we were alone. But now that idiot Puttaswamy was there. And it was not as if I could have stopped him from noticing her tears. It was after all a small room that *The Narasimhapura Post* called its office and not some Central Station. Nor was she being very subtle about it. When I said she burst into tears you mustn't get the impression that the tears were flowing silently or even that she was making an attempt to keep quiet about it. She was actually creating a racket. She began with a few sniffs but within a matter of seconds she reached a pitch that would have done a Hindustani vocalist proud. Then she started beating her breast and banging her head against the typewriter.

I was now beginning to get worried. The racket she was creating was bound to be heard on the road outside, and with the streets being so tense, the policemen patrolling the streets could have reached all kinds of conclusions. And with their fingers nervously massaging the triggers of their rifles, anything could have happened. In a desperate effort to calm her down I put my hands on her shoulders and rubbed her back.

'Don't make passes at a married lady,' Puttaswamy said in a tone that was so moralistic I could have killed him, if I hadn't been so surprised at hearing that tone from him. Puttaswamy normally behaved as if Rajalakshmi did not exist. And the few times he had spoken to her he had been quite curt, once even suggesting that the best way to get even if her husband was having an affair, was to have one herself. You would hardly expect someone like that to object to an elderly gentleman comforting a young girl.

'Don't be an idiot,' I said. 'Can't you see I am just trying to comfort this poor girl?'

'You may think you are comforting her, but to me it looks as if you are making a pass at her.'

'How dare you, you...' I stuttered. 'She is like my daughter.'

'If that is the way you were going to pat your daughter, it is lucky you didn't have one.'

This was getting to be too much. The fellow had been behaving strangely recently. The other day I had seen him staring out of the window for half an hour though the street outside was empty. But I was damned if I was going to let him take liberties with me. On top of everything, I didn't have to take rubbish from this idiot.

'Listen, you scoundrel!' I shouted, 'I don't know how you behave with women, but any idiot can see the girl needs to be calmed.'

'That is what I would like to know. What did you do to her that she needs to be calmed?'

'I will have you thrown out of this office if you...'

I don't know what I would have said or done if Rajalakshmi hadn't finally decided to interrupt us.

'Shut up!' she screamed at Puttaswamy. 'Sir is like a God to me. Don't you dare say such things about him.'

Puttaswamy just shrugged his shoulders, but I could see from the way his ears went red that this was not what he had expected.

'Well if you like it...' he said as he went back to reading some silly book.

Rajalakshmi would normally have picked up her slipper and thrown it at him for a comment like that. It was well known that she had a pretty good arm, which was why Puttaswamy was using the book more as a shield than actually reading it.

But to my surprise she did nothing of the kind. She just sat quietly with her shoulders hunched. It was as if the energy she had expended in my defence was all that she could manage. I sat down in front of her with my elbows on the table and waited patiently. After a couple of minutes she stopped sniffing long enough to say, 'He didn't come home last night.'

'Who?' It was a stupid question for she was obviously

talking about Mohan. But I couldn't think of anything else to say.

'Mohan,' she said. 'I waited the whole night and he did not come. He finally came in at 8 o'clock in the morning. He refused to tell me where he had been. Even after I gave him hot coffee he did not tell me. And after I made him some of my best dosas, I asked him again and he did not say anything. His mother then asked him and again he did not reply. It was not as if I did not know where he had been. He must have spent the night with that slut. But I had to hear it from him. So when he was leaving again I asked him directly whether he had been with Savitri that night and he did not deny it. In fact he said in a way I was right.'

And she began to wail again.

'This is a lie!' Puttaswamy thundered.

Things were now getting too confusing for me. I had first been surprised by Puttaswamy's interest in Rajalakshmi's crying. He hardly ever had time for anything she said or did. I was surprised even more by his moralistic tone when he accused me of making a pass at her. And now I couldn't understand just why he of all people should defend Mohan.

'What do you mean he was not with Savitri? Do you know where he was then?'

'How the hell should I know where he was?'

'You just said you knew.'

'I said nothing of the kind. All I said was I knew that he was not with Savitri.'

'How can you be so sure?' I asked, still perplexed.

'Because I spent the whole night with her.'

Just like that. He didn't try to hide it. He didn't blush. Nothing. He said he had spent the night with her as if it was the most normal thing to do. If anything, there was a touch of pride in it. He had the air of someone who would protect all womankind.

But I couldn't be bothered with some young idiot who had fallen in love. I just needed to get Rajalakshmi calm enough to take her to Krishnappa's place.

'Come, come,' I told her. 'Now you know Mohan did not spend the whole night with Savitri.'

'But he told me so,' she wailed.

'He must have just meant he spent some time with her, that's all.'

This only made her wail even louder.

'Look at that slut, she has two men after her at the same time. And Mohan even prefers sharing her to having the whole of me.'

This outburst was too much for Puttaswamy to take. He may have been feeling protective towards all womanhood, but that did not mean he would allow such statements to be made about his lady love.

'Mind what you say,' he snapped at Rajalakshmi, jumping out of his chair. 'Savitri is too good to even look at your stupid small-town husband. He must be just using her name as a cover for the kind of women he normally sleeps with.'

This time Rajalakshmi was true to form. In one smooth action she picked up her slipper and threw it at Puttaswamy with an accuracy that would have made the Nawabs of Pataudi, both senior and junior, jealous. Puttaswamy, true to form, ducked into the throw, getting the slipper square on the temple. Not for the first time was I thankful that Rajalakshmi always wore rubber slippers. I moved quickly between the two of them.

'Come along,' I told her, 'let's go, let's go'.

'Where?' she asked.

'To Krishnappa's place. He is the only one who can tell you where Mohan really was.'

'But Mohan does not talk to him any more.'

'I know, but Krishnappa will definitely know everything about him.'

She had no difficulty accepting that. Everybody in Narasimhapura knew that Krishnappa always knew everything that happened here. It was a common joke in Narasimhapura that Krishnappa knew the sex of a child even before its parents. He had a network of informants who kept him posted about every little inconsequential event in town. It was obvious that he would have kept track of Mohan's activities, especially if he had broken away from him. After Puttaswamy had regained enough chivalry to return Rajalakshmi's slipper, I opened the door for her and we walked briskly to Krishnappa's house.

▲ 6 ▼

THE MOMENT WE STEPPED OUT OF THE OFFICE WE COULD FEEL the tension on the streets. Almost all the shops had downed their shutters. Even the tin shack at the corner of Siddappa Lane that sold cigarettes, usually the last to close and the first to open, was doing business only through a half-open window. The normally busy road was almost completely empty except for clusters of policemen sitting tensely on the steps of the closed shops. The atmosphere was absolutely still but for the stray dogs running around. The eeriness was heightened by the large number of faces peering down from terraces and first floor windows, almost willing something to happen. The occasional pedestrians, compelled by some pressing matter to leave the security of their homes, were walking briskly, casting furtive glances to either side of the road, particularly at the intersection that cut into Mahatma Gandhi Road.

The atmosphere had evidently got to the policemen as

well. They were distinctly edgy. Whatever safety their numbers provided had been eroded by the uncertainty of unknown surroundings. The presence of so many guns in nervous hands was enough to put the fear of the unexpected into every citizen of Narasimhapura. It may have been this fear, or just the urge to find out where Mohan had been the previous night, that lent Rajalakshmi's step an urgency she rarely displayed.

I wasn't keen on strolling either. I wanted to get off the roads as quickly as possible. And Krishnappa's house was quite a distance away. It was at least fifteen minutes walk from the bus-stand on the road that led to one of the villages around Narasimhapura. His grandfather had bought the house from a British missionary who had had elaborate plans for Narasimhapura, that included building a school and a church on the land around the house. When the missionary suddenly left soon after Independence, Narayanappa had found the house large enough to match his status while also being unostentatious enough to match his Gandhian ideology. But it was not the best place to try to reach when the town was tense. You had to pass through the market, which is where most of the trouble begins in Narasimhapura. And anything could happen in the long, lonely stretch to Krishnappa's house. To make matters worse, just as we were passing the bus-stand, Rajalakshmi suddenly picked up a stone and threw it at a dog, muttering, 'That is the way she must be treated.' The dog yelped and the nervous policemen grabbed their rifles. Luckily they relaxed when they saw that Rajalakshmi and I were the only ones on the road. But it made me walk even more briskly, till I was almost running. We made it to Krishnappa's place in ten minutes, leaving me quite breathless as I gave her last minute instructions.

'You wait here,' I told her when we approached the wooden gate that led to the old colonial style bungalow. 'I will go into the house and explain the situation to Krishnappa.'

'No,' she said.

'No?' I looked at her incredulously as it was a word she rarely uttered to me. Over the years I had grown quite accustomed to hearing her agree with everything I said.

'No,' she repeated with a determined look on her face. 'I will not allow you to go inside. I know how much you hate Krishnappa. It was your greatness that you accompanied me till here after all that has happened between the two of you. But I will not allow you to be humiliated. And for you to walk into his house will be a humiliation.'

'Yes, yes, of course,' I told her. 'I know it is a humiliation. But your happiness is very much more important for me. This is a small sacrifice that I will gladly make for your sake.'

To my horror the look on her face only became more determined.

'No, Sir. You will not make any more sacrifices for my sake. The man I have given my whole life to has not bothered to treat me well. That is my karma. But I can't make up for that by forcing you to make sacrifices.'

This was getting ridiculous. The whole purpose of bringing the girl here was to break the ice with Krishnappa. And now here was the possibility that I would just stand outside his house while she went in.

'Don't be silly,' I told her with all the fatherliness I could manage, which wasn't much considering I was getting quite irritated with her behaviour. 'You are a young girl and I can't let you go inside the house by yourself. You don't know Krishnappa. He does not know how to behave with women. And he has all kinds of political riff-raff with him. They can do anything to you.'

'Let them, let them,' she said throwing open her arms with a gesture that owed a lot to her deep interest in Kannada commercial cinema. 'After all what more is there for me to lose now? A woman who has lost her husband has nothing more to lose. If there is a God above he will take care of me and if he doesn't, what is the point in living?'

With tears streaming down her face, clutching her thali in her right hand, she opened the gate and ran down the path that led to the front door of Krishnappa's house. For one brief, mad moment I considered running after her. But the group of five policemen who were patrolling the street were already taking a keen interest in our little scene in front of the gate. The sight of me running after a crying woman, that too a married one, was all that they would have needed to convince themselves that I was not up to any good. And the last thing *I* needed was another brush with the police.

As I stood nervously at the gate, Rajalakshmi banged her fists on the door with an urgency that must have got across to those on the other side of it. She had hardly been at it for half a minute when a window was opened tentatively and as soon as it became clear that it was a lady the door was opened quickly. Rajalakshmi had barely entered when it was shut again. But in that brief moment I could see that it was Krishnappa's mother who had come to the door. Just my luck I thought, with the old lady around, Rajalakshmi would have no problem telling her story and gaining sympathy, if not the information she wanted about her husband. The dim hope I had entertained that her nerve would fail and she would send for me had now disappeared.

It was with a sense of deep foreboding that I thought of the consequences of not meeting Krishnappa, not getting his side of the story, not having restored a balance in the next morning's paper, and not being able to avoid being arrested; and then my luck changed.

At the end of the road on which Krishnappa's house stood, there was a slum consisting of a cluster of huts. This cluster, in the middle of one of the Old Residents areas in Narasimhapura, had come up quite suddenly during an election two years ago. Krishnappa had at that time been wooing the Barkis to complement the strong support he had among the Old Residents. A rival politician had then brought in a group of Barkis to build their huts on a playground near Krishnappa's house. He had calculated that Krishnappa would be forced by the Old Residents to remove the slum, in the process putting paid to any chance he may have had of making inroads into Barki territory. Krishnappa had seen through the game and had tried to walk the tightrope by asking the Barkis to leave without actually removing the slum. But this had only resulted in him losing support among both the Old Residents and the Barkis. The slum had survived that election and the next, but it had become a political liability that Krishnappa would have loved to have removed, so long as the removal was not directly attributable to him.

As I stood outside his house bemoaning my bad luck, a couple of autorickshaws sped past me and screeched to a halt in front of the slum. From each vehicle poured out more well-built men than I would have thought was possible to fit into an autorickshaw. The lathis in their hands, the way they circled the huts and the fact that they were not Barkis, all told me that they did not belong to that slum. The one giving the orders appeared very familiar but I could not place him immediately. And as they set about what they had clearly come there for, identifying him was the last thing on my mind. They surrounded one of the huts. The leader then opened a can of kerosene and gave it to another who poured it on the roof and walls. He then dipped a piece of cloth into the kerosene and lit it with a match. When the cloth had caught fire he threw it on to the thatched roof. As the hut caught fire, a young couple ran out, straight into a series of lathi blows. The man was attacked first, and beaten up badly, till a blow to the back of the head felled him. As the woman screamed, her sari was pulled away from her and her blouse ripped apart. One of the men brought an old car tyre and put it around her neck. The leader then walked up to her and lit a match to the tyre. It was only when the tyre burst into flames that I realised with horror that it must have been soaked in kerosene.

The police patrol which had watched the scene with a detached air, suddenly sprang into action. A tear-gas gun appeared in the hands of one of the constables, who aimed at the clear blue sky on top of the huts and fired. The goondas got into the autorickshaws and disappeared as quickly as they had come. The screams of the woman as she died trying to get the burning tyre off her neck turned my blood to ice making me forget all my troubles. I just had to get out of that road and the only option I had was to enter Krishnappa's house. Any lingering doubts I may have had were removed by one of the policemen.

'What are you doing on the road!' the constable yelled. 'Why don't you go inside your house?'

'It is not my house!'

'Well, it will be your grave if you don't go in soon.'

I opened the gate and went in thinking I would stand behind the mango tree just inside the wall so that I would not attract either the attention of a mob or a stray police bullet. But just as I entered the gate, the door opened. The commotion on the road had evidently led Rajalakshmi to tell Krishnappa's mother that I was standing there. And the old lady immediately came to the door to call me in. With a sigh of relief I walked quickly to the door and shut it behind me.

▲▼

I took off my shoes in the verandah which was enclosed by a green wooden grill and walked into the drawing room. I had been there years ago before my relationship with Krishnappa had soured, but the room looked the same. It was still quite dark. The hexagonal ventilator near the roof did not provide much light as the roof was at least eighteen feet high. And the tubelight was still covered with dust. The water in the glass fish tank in one corner of the room was still quite dirty, though I suppose it must have been changed since the last time I was there. The radio that had been kept on the table at the other corner had, of course, been replaced by a television set, but that didn't make too much of a difference as it was covered with a piece of cloth similar to the one that used to cover the radio and had the same old metal flower vase with plastic flowers on top of it. Come to think of it Krishnappa's mother was now sitting on the same sofa on which she had been sitting when I was last there. And when she spoke now it was with the same righteous tone which had sometimes made me wonder whether Krishnappa's father had not done the right thing by staying away from home.

'Look what you have done!' she exclaimed.

I immediately looked around to see if I had upset something. My eyes instinctively went to the fish tank whose glass top I had cracked years ago by keeping a hot glass of coffee on it under the mistaken notion that it also served as a table. While I noticed the crack was still there, I knew even she could not possibly have been referring to that incident.

'Look what you have done!' she repeated even louder, leaving me quite perplexed.

'I have done nothing.'

'Nothing! You call this nothing? So many people being killed and you call it nothing?'

It was only then that I realised she was talking about the riots. The common perception that I was responsible for the whole thing suited her need for a daily dose of issues to be righteous about. I had a good mind to tell her that I had nothing to do with it and explain the entire circumstances under which that day's edition of *The Narasimhapura Post* had been brought out. But she was, as usual, in no mood to listen.

'You call it nothing when all these innocent people are dying. You have misled these poor ignorant people to go around killing each other.'

Well, there was nothing about the man I had just seen doing the killing to suggest that he would have been influenced by an English newspaper. I would have been surprised if he was able to read a paper in any language, let alone English. In fact, the more I thought of him the more I realised how stupid it was to believe that *The Narasimhapura Post* had anything to do with the riots. But then who could argue with idiots like that policeman Nanjappa or this crazy woman?

'Who has given you the right to take lives?' she

continued without letting me get a word in sideways. 'When I see these men killing each other I don't blame them. I blame people like you who make them do this to each other.'

I was not sure how much more of this I could take. I had to keep reminding myself that I just had to talk to Krishnappa, and what little chance I had of doing so would disappear if I displeased this mad old woman. But my anger was proving quite difficult to control. Anybody who saw what had happened outside the house would have realised that it was cold-blooded murder and not just something done in anger. Anybody who saw the face of the leader of that murdering gang would have realised that it was the face of a professional killer and not that of an innocent who couldn't control his rage. It was a face that you would not see in any respectable home. It was a face you would be surprised to find in any residential locality. It was the sort of face you would only find in those cheap bars. It was only in the dim light of those bars that the scar on his face could be ignored. It was a face that...

And then it suddenly struck me. It was a face that I had seen before. It was the face of the man I had seen coming out of the bar with the shadiest reputation in town. It was about a month ago when I was returning home late from the office. The only reason I had even looked in the direction of the bar was because I had seen Krishnappa coming out of it. And he was accompanied by the man who had done the killing near Krishnappa's house.

The sudden realisation made my knees weak. Here I was listening to this mad old lady giving me all this stupid rubbish about killing people, when all the while it was her son who was directly involved.

My first reaction was one of anger. I would show them just what a newspaper could do. I would expose them. I would carry a front page story proving that Krishnappa was behind the riots. I would carry more stories on the other pages all pointing a finger at Krishnappa. I would carry photographs of Krishnappa and the burnt huts. I would record Krishnappa's entire career, listing all his dubious deals.

The list of things I wanted to do with Krishnappa in the next day's paper was a long one, and by the time I had gone through that list some of my anger had passed. Once my thoughts were no longer confused by anger, it was quite obvious that all the things that I wanted to do had already been done in that morning's paper, and the only result had been a poke in the ribs from Nanjappa's stick and the threat of arrest. Though I now knew that that idiot Puttaswamy was right, there was still no way I could prove that Krishnappa was involved. And anybody who had seen the face of his hired murderer would have acknowledged that it would have been quite foolhardy to even contemplate giving evidence against him. With a sick feeling in my stomach I realised that I still needed to talk to Krishnappa and present his version in the next day's paper. And if I was to have any chance at all of meeting him I had to listen to all the rubbish that the old lady was pouring out.

'Mind you I am not saying anything about all that you have written about my poor boy,' she continued. 'Any other mother would have not let you into her house after what you have written about Krishnappa. Everyone knows what a gentle boy he is. When he was young, *I* had to kill the chickens we cooked because he couldn't stand the sight of blood. And you are trying to tell the whole world that he is behind this riot. Fortunately no one believes you. But you had better leave before he gets up. He will not be able to tolerate the sight of you in this room.'

'But I have to meet him,' I said.

'Are you mad? He will never forgive me if he knows I let you into the house.'

'But I must meet him to seek his forgiveness.' My tone had a touch of desperation.

The idea of my begging her son to forgive me seemed to appeal to her. 'You must touch his feet as soon as he enters the room.'

This was going far beyond my worst expectations. Was I destined to only keep touching the feet of younger men for the rest of my life? But then, what choice did I have?

Krishnappa's mother called the servant and asked him to inform her son that I had come to personally apologise to him. The servant returned with the message that Krishnappa had no intention of meeting me. The old lady then sent the servant back with the message that it was not polite to refuse to meet people who had come to the house. When the servant returned with the 'who the hell asked him to come?' message, the old lady sent him back, saying she had invited me in. Once Krishnappa had left no room for any doubt that he was not keen to meet me, he came into the room and sat down on the big armchair which had been used exclusively by his grandfather.

His mother looked at me as if to say, you said you would touch his feet. I swallowed my pride and walked up to him and bowed to touch his feet. He did nothing to stop me. Instead his face broke into a huge grin.

'It is all right,' he said. 'In spite of all that you have done to hurt me over the years I have never held a grudge against you. I will not deny that this morning's paper hurt me. But I am not a petty man. I forgive you.'

'Thank you,' I mumbled.

'It is all right. It is all right. Nanjappa told me that you will be correcting all those silly articles that you had published. I personally don't care what the papers write about me. God and my mother know the truth. It is just these other boys who get so upset when I am unfairly attacked.'

'I am sorry, it will not happen again.'

'Of course, I know it will not happen again. Nanjappa told me that you will balance all that was written about me today.'

'Yes, yes. I will carry an apology saying that all those stories were baseless. And I will carry other stories saying that you are not involved in the riots.'

'That is not balance. You have attacked me one day, and just because you stop attacking me you think you have restored balance? What kind of justice is that?'

'What do you want then?'

'I want articles supporting the Old Residents. After all Narasimhapura is their town. How can these Barkis come from somewhere and take it away. Just because we are hospitable they shouldn't take advantage of it. They shouldn't mistake our tolerance for weakness.'

I couldn't help thinking about the tolerance level of the man who had lit the tyre around the woman's neck. But I quickly put such rash thoughts out of my mind.

'Of course, you are right. We must not allow others to misuse our tolerance. Just because we are such kind-hearted people our children should not grow up thinking that they should not be proud of being Old Residents.'

I took great care to emphasise the 'we'. I didn't want

him clubbing me with the Barkis simply because I was not born in Narasimhapura.

'You will, of course, also have to balance the articles at a personal level.'

'What personal level?' I asked him.

'You carried an article attacking me personally.'

'Yes, yes, I am sorry about that. We will carry another article pointing out all your glorious contributions to Narasimhapura.'

'What use will that be? I can publish any number of good stories about myself. But you have belittled my position by making it look as if that woman is the main politician in this town. That is what you must balance.'

'You mean you want an article attacking Savitri?'

'I only want the truth. You think the character of a girl like that can be good? She is living all alone. Who knows what she does at night? What about all those boys who come to see her from Bangalore? And I will tell you one thing that I have not told anybody else because I do not malign women. Her father and mother do not live together anymore. Can such a woman be the main politician of Narasimhapura? Is it not your duty to inform the poor people of Narasimhapura about her true character?'

'Yes, yes, of course it is. I will personally see that an article is written about her.'

Before he could make any further demands I said 'Namaskara Amma' to his mother and was about to leave when Rajalakshmi suddenly piped up, 'What about me?'

In all the excitement I had completely forgotten about her and her problems with Mohan.

'Why don't you ask him where Mohan was last evening?' I said nodding towards Krishnappa.

'How will I know where he was?' Krishnappa said.

'We only want to know if he was with Savitri.' Rajalakshmi's voice almost choked over that name.

'With Savitri?' Krishnappa seemed genuinely surprised. 'I don't know where he was and I don't care.'

His tone was curt enough to make even Rajalakshmi realise that she would not get any information from him. With a sniff she got up and bowed to touch the old lady's feet. I quickly escorted her out.

▲ 7 ▼

THE TENSION ON THE STREET WAS PALPABLE. THE FIRE IN THE Barki hutments was still raging. Narasimhapura's only fire engine had reached the spot, but the firemen were still busy trying to plug a leak in the hose. The body of the woman who had been burnt to death was lying in the middle of the road with the burnt tyre around her neck. The streets were empty but for the policemen standing near the hutments, waiting for the firemen to repair their hose. The tension had got across even to the stray dogs; one of them sat in the middle of the road, howling at the sky.

To step out at that moment had its risks. The tension on the streets would prompt anyone with a gun to fire first and think later, and the policemen would not have found it difficult to justify opening fire at a time like this. At the very least they would have been expected to arrest anyone who stepped out. As someone who has always been committed to the principle that discretion is the better part of valour, my instinct in such situations is to stay in hiding until the tension has eased. But that option was clearly not open to me. If I stayed any longer in Krishnappa's place there was no telling what further conditions would be imposed upon me. I had to step out hoping that the presence of a woman would curb the bloodthirsty instincts of the policemen. And if I was given a chance to speak before the first bullet was fired I could use my journalistic credentials to get a safe passage home. With a prayer on my lips, and taking care to keep Rajalakshmi between the group of policemen near the hutments and me, I opened the gate and we stepped out on to the road.

As luck would have it, at that very moment a police jeep came speeding from the other side. I was concentrating so intently on the policemen near the hutments that I didn't hear the vehicle till it screeched to a stop just behind me. With a start I turned around with my hands held up in front of my face, as if that could prevent a bullet from striking my head. I immediately started screaming 'I am a journalist, I am a journalist!' At least I thought I started screaming, though Rajalakshmi insists that while my lips were moving no sound came out of my throat.

'If the two of you want to flirt, why don't you do it inside your office?'

It was Nanjappa's voice. I would never have dreamt, especially after what had transpired in the office that morning, that I would ever have been happy to hear that voice. But at that moment there was no voice that could have made me happier. If I was to have any chance at all of explaining my presence on the road opposite Krishnappa's house in the middle of a riot, it was to someone who was aware of the urgency of my need to meet Krishnappa. And no one knew more about the need for this meeting than Nanjappa.

As I slowly lowered my hands and peeped out from above them, I could see that Nanjappa had stepped out of the jeep and was giving me a comforting smile. It was a smile that told me that he understood. He had been in Narasimhapura long enough to recognise how much of an effort it would have taken me to meet Krishnappa. As I saw the smile the tension slowly eased out of my body.

Don't get me wrong. The sight of Nanjappa's smile would not normally have caused any relief. His smile was not one that would have shortlisted him in the preliminary rounds of a beauty contest among baboons. It consisted of spreading his lips wide, baring a set of large yellow teeth that protruded from his dark, oily face. It was not a sight you would like young children to see. In fact, those who were not fond of Nanjappa—and he certainly wasn't the most popular man in Narasimhapura—used to say that he had had an unhappy childhood only because his parents feared the sight of his smile. But beauty, as they say, lies in the eyes of the beholder and at that moment his smile was a thing of beauty to me.

He curtly told the two of us to get into the back of his jeep while he himself walked over to the group of policemen near the still-burning hutments, evidently to discuss some matters of importance with them.

As we waited for him to return Rajalakshmi decided she had kept quiet for too long. 'Would you ever have thought,' she said staring at the burning huts, 'that people who have lived together for so many years would do this to each other; that they would treat each other so cruelly?'

Coming from Rajalakshmi this was a bit unusual. She was not one to normally comment on larger social issues. She rarely spoke about anything other than her husband or children and her attitude to her work at *The Narasimhapura Post* was closer to that of a casual observer than an employee. But then, I thought, what had happened over the last couple of days was enough to stir anybody's social consciousness. The sight of the contorted body of the woman with the still-smouldering tyre around her neck in the middle of the road would have touched the most cold-blooded of human beings.

'There are times when such things cannot be avoided,' I said in the most comforting tone I could manage.

'But when people have shared everything how can they turn around and hurt each other so much?'

The hurt in her eyes made me wonder if I should tell her that the woman lying dead on the road was not killed by anyone she knew, but by a goonda hired by Krishnappa. But I wasn't sure if Rajalakshmi could keep a secret. And, in any case, while this may have been a case of premeditated murder, the stories of some of the other rioting in Narasimhapura were full of old neighbours turning against each other. Just two streets from Krishnappa's house a young, educated boy had killed his cousin because he was seen going out with a Barki girl.

'I suppose,' I said, trying to find some method in the madness, 'people can only hurt those who are close to them at the time when their anger goes out of control.'

'But surely there must be some compassion towards someone you have known for years?'

Her use of the word compassion, I must admit, shook me a bit. It was not a word that was commonly used in Narasimhapura these days. I suppose Krishnappa's grandfather might have had some use for it, but I am sure if Krishnappa had tried being compassionate he would have left his followers quite confused. Some of them might even have doubted his motives. Within *The Narasimhapura Post* too I couldn't remember when compassion had been a factor in decision-making. I, for one, wouldn't have dared justify a decision to Bhimanna on the grounds that I was being compassionate. The few employees of his arrack business who had tried asking him to decide some issues on compassionate grounds were rudely reminded that it was he, and not some saint, who was their employer.

'Compassion is very important,' I told Rajalakshmi, 'but in times of anger people tend to forget it.'

'What has he got to be angry about?' she asked. 'In spite of all that he has done I have never said anything. If anyone should be angry it should be me.'

This went completely over my head. I didn't think she was directly involved in the riots in any way.

'Just what are you talking about?' I asked her.

'Why, about Mohan and me, of course,' she seemed mildly surprised. 'Just what did you think I was talking about all this while?'

Well, at least it showed that the riots had not, as yet, gone far enough to affect Rajalakshmi's view of the world. Whether any riot would ever be able to change her view of the world was, of course, debatable. But I had more important things on my mind than to worry about Rajalakshmi. It was one thing to promise to publish two articles along the lines Krishnappa wanted, but it was quite another to get the articles written. Krishnappa had left no room for doubt that he would only be satisfied with articles that were comparable in size to those that had appeared that morning. I couldn't think of anyone I could approach in the midst of a riot to come up with such large pieces on time.

The more I thought about it the more I was convinced that there was only one way out. I just had to follow the methods adopted by Puttaswamy, in putting together the next morning's edition of the paper.

By the time Nanjappa dropped us at the office with a curt 'Ok you can get out now,' my mind was made up. I would follow exactly the same methods used by Puttaswamy. I would write both articles. The one on Savitri could be attributed to a staff reporter. The other article on the historically just nature of the Old Residents' cause would be by Dr. Samuel Johnson. The hint that the expert may be a foreigner would surely carry more weight than Puttaswamy's pseudonym. It was about time the young fool realised that anything he could do, I could do better.

Writing the two pieces took me much less time than I thought it would. I always knew the piece on Savitri would be simple. There were a lot of stories I knew about her that would make people in Narasimhapura tap their fingers on their open mouths. I began with a rather innocuous one about how she had always refused to wear saris and then suddenly decided to wear nothing else when she entered Narasimhapura's politics. I then went on to the one about how she had walked out of her father's house because she was not allowed to cook beef in that Brahmin household, and only returned when she was assured that she could have all the beef she wanted. The story about Savitri and the postman then followed. This was a particular favourite of mine and I spent a lot of time detailing how, when she had been in high school, she had secretly met the postman every afternoon under a tree behind her parents' place. When they found out about it her parents were quite upset until they realised that the only reason she met the postman was because he provided her with her daily quota of cigarettes. And by the time I rounded off the piece with the story about her breaking her engagement with a boy from a respectable family simply because her parents had taken the decision without asking her, I was enjoying writing the piece so much that I regretted having to finish it. I was quite sure it would generate the required response. It was not as if such things were not heard of in Narasimhapura. Venkatappa's wife, Lakshman's daughter and even Saroja, the wife of the temple priest, were all characters whose exploits kept the conversation going for many an evening in Bhimanna's bars. But all of them at least went through the motions of keeping things secret. None of them behaved as if what they did, did not concern others. They all knew what happened to Lakshminarasimhaiah when he stopped making a distinction between what he did and what he pretended to be doing. For twenty-five years he had kept a woman and fathered three boys. The whole of Narasimhapura, including his wife and legitimate children, knew about it. But after his wife died, when he decided to bring the woman home all hell broke loose. The whole town behaved as if it was the first time they were hearing about the affair. They hounded him and his three illegitimate sons so viciously that the three boys had to leave Narasimhapura and get jobs in Bangalore. And soon Lakshminarasimhaiah and his woman went to live with them. Savitri either did not know this aspect of Narasimhapura or did not care. When someone had mentioned the story of her meetings with the postman she had only laughed aloud, without even pretending to be hurt. If she reacted the same way to my piece there was no doubt that whatever sympathy she may have had in Narasimhapura would be a thing of the past.

The second article giving the expert opinion was the one I was worried about. I had never met an expert, let alone read anything written by one. I decided to take the easy way out by simply following what Puttaswamy had written about how the Barkis were in reality older residents than the Old Residents. And the pattern turned out to be a lot simpler than I had thought it would be. All I had to do was pretend I was dealing with a very complicated matter, rather like my astrologer did when I asked him to predict the outcome of specific problems that I was facing. Once I had adopted the right tone I only had to support my strong assertions by quoting someone or the other. It didn't take me long to get started. 'While the question of the exact point at which the deity of the local temple was found depends on whether future evidence substantiates what is already known, there is no doubt that the Res-Barki rests on a foundation containing a stone from the rock where the deity was found.' From then on it was only a question of finding enough names to quote. Puttaswamy had quoted a series of foreign experts, but I did not need to do so since I had made the author a foreigner. I sent the story to the press well in time and walked home briskly before it got dark. The odd paan shop in the streets off Mahatma Gandhi Road was open, but I still did not want to risk walking slowly in the night until full normalcy had returned.

The next morning I left home early. Whatever Savitri may have thought of the article on her, she could not have been happy about the other article stating a viewpoint diametrically opposed to her own. And when Savitri did not agree with something published in *The Narasimhapura Post* there was only one way in which she would respond: organise a dharna in front of the office. She would come there leading a procession consisting mostly of women. They would be carrying placards with slogans on the specific issue they were protesting against and one large worn-out placard stating in bold, red letters, 'Workers Unity Zindabad'. Her dharnas were perfectly planned and followed a distinct pattern from which she rarely deviated as every little detail had a reason. The dharna would begin at 10.30 in the morning as her followers had to first pack and send tiffin boxes to their husbands. They would then gather outside Lakshmi Talkies so that they passed the local police station before turning into Mahatma Gandhi Road on the way to the office of *The Post*. When they walked past the police station they would make sure to cause more noise than you would have thought possible from a group of fifteen women. Once they were sure that a group of policemen would follow them they would proceed towards the office.

It would normally take them about five minutes to reach the office unless they were delayed at the police station because there were no constables available to follow them immediately. But since the constables rarely had anything else to do, and quite liked the idea of walking behind a group of women, these delays were rare. Once they reached the office they would sit on the steps raising slogans for about ten to fifteen minutes. The constables would then climb up the stairs and stand in front of the door so as to prevent anyone from entering the office. After the constables were in place the women would make a formal attempt at breaking the police cordon. Since the stairs were quite narrow, not more than three of them could charge at the constables at a time. They would keep pushing themselves against the young policemen in groups of three. After they had all had their turn, and it was clear to the meanest intelligence that they were causing more pleasure than pain to the able-bodied young constables, they would troop out with the satisfaction of a good day's work having been done.

The ritual was quite harmless as long as everything went according to plan. But if for some reason, there was even a slight change in the sequence of events, the women tended to panic, and things could go very wrong. Once I was not in the office when the dharna team arrived. Finding the office locked they did not know which door to charge into. After a while they decided to charge down the steps and out of the door they had just entered. At the same time the constables were trying to make their way up the stairs. In the confusion one of the constables tripped and fell down the stairs. Being a policeman, he naturally did not want to fall alone. He spread his arms out as he fell, taking two of the women down with him. As the women started screaming rape at the top of their shrill voices the other policemen panicked and took to their heels. Seeing his comrades deserting him the policeman on the ground panicked as well and picking up his lathi started swinging it about. The women ran in all directions trying to find hidden doors that would allow them to escape from the small stairway. In the process they broke more glass panes than they realised and the remaining were broken by the constable who kept swinging his lathi well after the women had left. It had taken me a great deal of effort to calm Bhimanna down when he had seen the mess. And with the prevailing tension in the town the last thing I wanted was for the dharna to follow any pattern even slightly different from the usual.

When I left home it was only 8.30—well before the normal dharna time. But I was not taking any chances. And, in any case, I had to go to Rajalakshmi's place on the way. I always went to her house on a dharna day to warn her not to come to the office. If she did she would invariably get into a fight with one of the women. The women saw her as someone desperately in need of liberation and she strongly objected to anyone trying to liberate her from her film magazines. And if she got hysterical inside the office when the other women were screaming outside, things could get out of hand.

Even as I entered the lane on which Rajalakshmi lived I could hear a faint wail. At first I could not make out where it was coming from. As the front doors of all the houses on both sides of that narrow lane opened out directly on to the street, with very little distance between them, it was difficult to spot the house from which the noise was coming. It was only when I had almost reached the front door of Rajalakshmi's house, after taking care to avoid the rubbish and the pools of stagnant water on the once-tarred road, that I realised it was her voice. I quickened my step and entered the house through the open door on the street. Rajalakshmi was sitting on the floor in a corner of the room clutching a piece of red cloth in her hands. Tears were streaming down her cheeks as her mother-in-law held her, trying to comfort her.

'What happened?' I asked. I got no reply because it was impossible for anyone to have heard my voice over Rajalakshmi's racket.

'What happened?' I asked again at the top of my

voice. This time I had taken care to speak during the short interval between her wails when Rajalakshmi paused for breath.

But that didn't help very much. From the way she stared at me with her eyes wide open, I knew she had heard me. But all she did was to thrust the red cloth out at me and launch into another loud wail.

At Rajalakshmi's next pause for breath it was her mother-in-law who spoke, 'It's Mohan.'

The tone in which she said it, followed by Rajalakshmi's loudest wail yet, made me fear the worst. The fact that the streets were deserted in the morning, after some of the paan shops had opened the previous evening, was a clear indication that there had been trouble last night. With Mohan now tending to stay out late, if not being away the whole night, it was always possible he had been in the wrong place at the wrong time. And in the tension that prevailed in Narasimhapura these days no one who stumbled into the violence could hope to get out alive.

The very thought of Mohan being killed during the riot touched a chord deep inside me. Much as I disapproved of the way he had treated Rajalakshmi the last few days, I could not forget that he was one of Narasimhapura's brightest hopes. So much was expected of him even when he was in school. And, as he had grown up and started working, all of us in Narasimhapura were proud of his achievements.

'How did it happen?' I asked, sitting down on the red oxide floor in front of Rajalakshmi.

'How should I know,' Rajalakshmi wailed. 'But I knew it had to happen.'

'How did you find out about it?' I tried again.

'When I found this,' she said brandishing the red cloth again. As she waved it in front of my face I could see that it wasn't just a cloth but a blouse.

'Where did you find this?' I asked as patiently as I could.

'In the suitcase,' she said, as if that was the silliest question she had ever heard.

I took a deep breath and tried again, 'Which suitcase?'

'The suitcase he brought home with him this morning, what other suitcase would I be talking about?'

'Who brought the suitcase?' I rasped, getting quite exasperated.

'Why Mohan, of course,' she said.

I was now completely confused. 'You mean to say Mohan came home this morning?'

'Yes.'

'Then what is all this crying about?'

'About this,' she wailed waving the red blouse again.

'That is just a blouse,' I shouted. 'What is there in that silly blouse to make you cry as if someone is dead?'

'You don't understand,' she cried. 'It is her blouse.'

I just couldn't take much more of this. But I had to know what the hell was happening. 'Whose blouse?'

'Savitri's, of course. He came home this morning with a suitcase. When I asked him whose it was he said it was Savitri's. He didn't even have the decency to pretend that it was not hers. And when he left immediately afterwards I asked him where he was going and he said he was going to Savitri's place.'

'Are you trying to tell me that you are creating all this drama only because Mohan brought a suitcase home?'

'But it wasn't just any suitcase. After he left I opened it.

And it was full of all kinds of funny clothes. This blouse was the only decent thing in it.'

'But he could have just been carrying her suitcase for her. There is nothing wrong in that.'

'I knew you would say something like that. You are always trying to comfort me. That is your greatness. But there is no need for it. Whatever is my karma I have to live with it.'

There was no point talking to her. I just sat around a while longer as my presence seemed to calm her down at least a little. After some time when she stopped wailing and began to cry rather more silently, I got up and told her not to come to the office.

▲ 8 ▼

As I walked to the office I thought how sensible it had been to leave home early. The visit to Rajalakshmi's house had taken much longer than I had anticipated, and there was more trouble when I was crossing the market on the way back to Mahatma Gandhi Road. A speeding police jeep had lost control while turning into the market and had rammed into a cigarette kiosk at the corner. The kiosk had overturned, taking its owner who was sitting inside, down with it. Fortunately, he was not badly hurt. But for those peeping out of their first-floor windows, the sight of a dishevelled cigarette-seller being surrounded by a large number of armed policemen was easy to misinterpret. And by the time the story had travelled from one first-floor window to another and reached the next street, it had become one about the police attacking the cigarette-seller because he had dared to open his kiosk. It was in this form that I heard it and my first reaction was to avoid the entire area. But since I had to cross the market to get to the office, I decided instead to chat up a few policemen. Once I had told them I was a journalist, they were not only willing to escort me past the market but also gave me their version of what had happened. By the time I finally reached the office it was ten o'clock.

There was just enough time to read that morning's paper before Savitri was to arrive with her activists for the dharna. I settled down in my chair and read the piece I had written on her. It made very entertaining reading, even if I say so myself. In fact, I enjoyed it so much that I kept reading it again and again. When I was finally satisfied I looked up at the old wall clock and was a bit surprised to find it showing eleven o'clock, which meant that it was now ten forty-five. Savitri had evidently been delayed. It must be the tension in the town, I thought. It would have given the lunch-man an excuse to take it easy. And the women in Savitri's brigade would have had to wait until he came and collected the lunch-boxes that they had packed for their husbands.

Having already read the paper I had to look for other things to do. It just wouldn't do to be sitting idle when Savitri arrived. She would invariably have enough nasty things to say without my providing her with more ammunition. I picked up some old copies of *The Narasimhapura Post* that were lying in a corner and began clipping them. Ever since Puttaswamy had joined the paper he had been talking about the need for a clipping service for the paper. I had told Bhimanna then it was just one of those silly expensive ideas that immature youngsters were bound to come up with and there was nothing the clipping service could provide that I couldn't clip myself. I had not quite found the time to clip anything regularly, but if clippings were what impressed these young fools, so be it.

It took me fifteen minutes to cut up the first paper. When Savitri failed to show up even after I had finished clipping it I was a bit worried. I didn't want her to delay the dharna too long. With so much work for the policemen in the town they were most likely to be free only in the morning. If she delayed it too long, and the policemen couldn't come, we would both be stuck at the dharna without knowing how to end it. And there was no telling what would happen if Savitri and her maids got tired of waiting. It was with a touch of nervousness that I began clipping the second paper.

I took a while longer over this, cutting the longer stories into two and marking them 'Part 1' and 'Part 2'. But even after I had finished cutting the paper into as many pieces as possible there was no sign of Savitri. I paced up and down the small office, peering out of the window at regular intervals. Unable to control my nervousness I picked up the third paper and began clipping it. Actually, since my mind was not on the job, I wonder if you could say I was clipping it. It was more like cutting it into shreds. After a while I even stopped using the scissors and tore it with my bare hands. I was getting quite worked up by now. It was thus quite a relief when I heard the sounds of slogans being shouted at a distance.

The relief didn't last long, for even when the shouting was far away, I could make out that there was something quite different about the slogans that were being raised. As the group came closer the differences became very obvious. To begin with, this was not a group of women activists. As they turned the corner from Mahatma Gandhi Road, I could see that the group was, in fact, entirely male. Instead of carrying placards attacking me and *The Narasimhapura Post*, they were waving copies of the day's edition of the paper. And instead of shouting slogans against the paper or me, they were shouting slogans in my favour. The rustic slogans they had coined may have made a less experienced man than myself blush, but there was no denying that they were in my favour.

As the group came to the door of the office I could make out that they were led by Thimanna, the youngster who had challenged Savitri at the peace meeting. He was, as usual, very simply but neatly dressed with his shirt tucked properly into pants that hugged his skinny legs. His large bright eyes seemed larger than usual as he led the crowd of what were clearly Krishnappa's men. They were all well-built and had the manner of a group of bulls who could be made to charge on command. As soon as I saw the crowd and the mood they were in, my attitude to Savitri's dharna changed. The last thing I now wanted was for the women to come early. I didn't dare think of what could happen if Savitri's maids arrived before I had got rid of these muscular young men. I rushed down the stairs determined to finish with these young men as quickly as I could.

'Thank you, thank you,' I said even before I reached the door and kept repeating the two words when I went outside.

The group greeted my presence with a loud cheer.

'I am grateful for the support you have given me and *The Narasimhapura Post* at this critical hour,' I told them. 'I am indebted to all of you for the way you have taken time off to come here and appreciate quality journalism.

But it wouldn't be fair on my part to take too much of your time, so please go home.'

I couldn't have got to the point much faster than that. But it didn't seem to help. The group showed no sign of dispersing. Instead, they sat on the road and Thimanna came up to stand beside me and raised his hands indicating he wanted silence.

'We have not come here to go away without showing you our true feelings,' Thimanna began. 'You can see what has happened to our country because those who are honest have preferred to keep quiet. If all honest men had worked together we would not have allowed such a corrupt society to come about. But now the attitude of the youth has undergone a change. We will no longer keep quiet. We will show the world that we cannot be bullied any longer. People cannot make use of our traditional tolerance. We have come here to support you. What kind of men would we be if we let Old Residents who have built our great town stand alone at this time of crisis. Can we say we don't have the time to fight for a just cause? What are a few hours in the cause of justice? We will sacrifice a thousand hours for quality journalism. We will sacrifice a thousand days for quality journalism.'

The group began to cheer, making it clear that they wanted more of the same. And Thimanna was more than willing to provide it.

'We will sacrifice a thousand years for the cause of quality journalism,' he said. And realising that each of them did not have a thousand years to sacrifice, he changed track. 'We will sacrifice a thousand lives for quality journalism. Blood will flow on the streets of Narasimhapura in aid of quality journalism.'

I didn't know quality journalism was such a major concern, but evidently it was. Thimanna made it sound an objective well worth sacrificing for. And the rest of the group, possibly because most of them were illiterate, seemed to agree.

'Quality journalism Zindabad! Zindabad, Zindabad! Quality journalism Zindabad! Zindabad, Zindabad!' The chant, which was loud enough to begin with, rose to a crescendo.

And then my worst fears came true.

Turning in from Mahatma Gandhi Road was another group led by Savitri, with her right index finger pointing, as always, to the skies. With Thimanna's group still shouting loudly, I could not hear what her group was screaming. But from the manner in which their hands went up and down in unison it was clear that they were chanting slogans too. And I didn't need great insight to realise that the slogans would not be in my favour.

The first thought that crossed my mind as soon as I saw the crowd approach was how to keep the two groups from clashing. The rustic crowd that Thimanna had brought with him could be trusted to laugh rather than get provoked by the aggressiveness of the women with Savitri. But as her group came closer I saw, to my dismay, that it did not consist only of women. There were also a fair number of men there. And among the more vociferous male slogan shouters walking in the first row, next to Savitri, was Mohan.

In the group that Savitri had gathered, Mohan stood out quite sharply. Her group had an informal uniform with the women in cotton saris and the men in pyjamas and kurtas. Mohan, on the other hand, had not bothered to change his normal attire. His black shoes were polished to the point where they glinted in the sun. His white polyester trousers were spotless. The shine on his broad black belt matched that on his shoes, just as his crimson T-shirt was in sharp contrast to the deliberately sober colours of Savitri's sari.

I ran down the narrow lane quickly to stand between the two groups, though what I could have done in case they had decided to go for each other, I do not know. As the group came close to Thimanna's men they seemed to be looking for a fight. The focus of their slogans shifted from me to Krishnappa. And some of the slogans they raised about Krishnappa wouldn't have been printed in a yellow journal let alone a paper of the stature of *The Narasimhapura Post*. The fact that it was the women who were screaming these slogans the loudest appeared to keep the rustic men from retaliating, but Thimanna himself was getting quite red in the face. As the slogans about Krishnappa became more vulgar, Thimanna was visibly finding it increasingly difficult to keep his self-control. After a particularly nasty but comprehensive one that cast aspersions on several members of Krishnappa's family his self-control, such as it was, broke down. He rolled up his sleeves and charged towards the women.

At that moment Mohan lifted his hand in the manner of a policeman stopping traffic, and Thimanna stopped. He stopped so suddenly that had he been operating on tyres I am sure there would have been a loud screech. The rest of Savitri's group must have been surprised by the effect that Mohan's gesture had, but they were too happy with the result to bother to think about it. Mohan cleared his throat to speak when Savitri raised her hand and silenced him.

'We have come here,' she began, but couldn't get much further as her voice was hoarse from all the slogan shouting.

She pointed towards Mohan, and it was then that I realised he was carrying Savitri's cloth bag on his shoulder. As if by reflex action he put his hand into the bag and came out with an old rum bottle full of water.

I couldn't help feeling a tinge of sadness. Here was this man who had such an influence over the youngsters of Narasimhapura that he could stop their indiscretions with a mere gesture, and he was reduced to carrying water for women. The way in which Savitri merely stretched her hand and expected to be served was too much for even a casual observer to take. Was this what we had showered so much affection on Mohan for? Was this the man the whole town was proud of? Was this the man who was supposed to bring glory to Narasimhapura? Some glory, running behind a woman with a water-bottle.

But I put such thoughts quickly out of my mind. This was not the time to stand around and ponder over the frailty of male self-respect and the power of woman. The possibility of a violent conflict was still there and I had to do something to disperse at least one of the groups. I thought my best chance was with Thimanna, since he was supposed to be on my side.

'Thank you for your support,' I told him. 'All of you must now be tired. So why don't you go and rest?'

It was a non-starter.

'What kind of people do you think we are?' Thimanna responded. 'Do you think we will go away and leave you alone with these...'

It may have sounded more polite if he had finished the sentence. With more hope than any realistic expectation I turned to Savitri, 'Now that you have made your point, why don't you go home and rest.'

'What makes you think I have made my point? We have not even begun. There are so many critical issues involved and you think you can get us out without our having had our say.'

'No, no, not at all,' I hastened to reassure her. 'The last thing I want is for you not to have your say. But since you have made your displeasure with me quite clear it might be better to take the rest of the say as said.'

'Who is concerned about you?' she asked with her fearsome clarity. 'The issues are much larger than any man, let alone an old duffer like you.'

Well, if the issues didn't concern me I didn't see the need to hold the show in front of my office. But I didn't dare tell her anything of the kind.

'The primary issue,' she continued, 'is how do we protect the secular character of Narasimhapura? Are we going to let a bunch of goondas destroy it? The answer is NO! We will protect the secular character of Narasimhapura to the last drop of our blood.'

These were fighting words, and it was lucky that most of Thimanna's crowd did not understand English, let alone when it was spoken with Savitri's accent.

'The second issue,' she said 'is how should Narasimhapura cope with the forces thrown up by social change? Are we going to let politicians tap these forces to build a fascist society? Are we going to accept a society in which all our freedom is lost? Are we going to accept a society where we cannot walk freely? The answer is NO! We will go to any extent to stop this from happening. We will make sure that all who support such causes lose their freedom. We will create a situation where they cannot walk freely on the streets of Narasimhapura. We will destroy their Goebbelian methods with the power of the people. History will see us triumph as we create a new social order on the ruins that were once the monuments of the Hitlerite parties.'

But it no longer seemed to matter whether the rest of the crowd understood English at all. Even those, like me, who knew the language so well didn't quite know what she was going on about. As she went on in the same vein all I could make out was that she knew a lot about the 1930s, especially about Germany. Which was pretty good for a young girl like her. Perhaps her father was posted there when she was young.

When she finally paused for breath, no one immediately knew what to say. But Thimanna realised he couldn't let her statement go unchallenged.

'All rubbish,' he said with refreshing simplicity.

Savitri must have been expecting a more complicated response than that, for she didn't quite know how to respond.

'All rubbish,' Thimanna repeated just in case she had not heard.

'What do you mean, 'all rubbish'?' she asked.

'All rubbish,' Thimanna answered, not willing to let the debate get out of hand.

'You must substantiate your case,' Savitri screamed. 'You cannot just say 'all rubbish' like that.'

'Yes, I can,' Thimanna said. And just to prove that he could, he repeated, 'all rubbish, all rubbish, all rubbish.'

Savitri was getting quite exasperated with this simple and direct attack.

'You do not know even the basics of social theory and you want to get into a debate?' Savitri's voice had now reached quite a high pitch. 'Why don't you read some books before you talk?'

'Why should I?' Thimanna responded. 'That is also rubbish.'

'Who are you to decide what is rubbish and what is not. What do you know about society to even understand what is rubbish. All the intelligent people of Narasimhapura do not think it is rubbish. You see Mohan here,' she said putting so friendly a hand on Mohan's shoulder that he blushed. 'Why can't you be like him. He is one of the most intelligent men in Narasimhapura and he has realised the value of what I have been saying all along.'

Thimanna seemed a bit taken aback by the mention of Mohan, but he had seen how effective his simple attack was and was not going to let go.

'I don't care what others think. Just because other people sell themselves it does not mean I will do so. Even if you charm every man in Narasimhapura I will stand alone. I am not afraid of saying what you have been speaking about is all rubbish. It may be in English, but it is still all rubbish.'

And as if to prove his point, he repeated, 'It's all rubbish, all rubbish, all rubbish.'

The crowd behind him decided that this was the new chant to be taken.

'All rubbish, all rubbish,' they began tentatively. Then one of the men at the back put the whole thing into a format they were familiar with.

'All rubbish, Zindabad!' he said.

'Zindabad, Zindabad!' the crowd responded.

With Thimanna's men shouting slogans, Savitri's group could not keep quiet. They went back to some of their more colourful slogans on Krishnappa. Since these were slogans that Thimanna's crowd could understand, it had an immediate effect. Some of the better built members of Thimanna's group lifted the lower ends of their dhotis and tied them tightly around their waists. They then made turbans out of their towels.

These signs of preparation for warfare sent a chill down my spine. Any violence between the two groups would cause considerable damage. The sloganeering had brought out a whole lot of interested onlookers, especially children who found it very entertaining to hear Savitri speak English. The jostling crowd, with excited children right in front, would have caused a stampede if any violence broke out. The policemen who were present in large numbers had so far remained spectators, but they would then have been forced to add violence of their own. I was fearing the worst, when all of a sudden the attention of the crowd shifted away from the amateur debaters to someone who was trying to make his or her way to the office.

From the manner in which the crowd was quietly parting to make way, it was clearly someone quite respected in Narasimhapura. Though the crowd was making way willingly enough, it was a while before the person came through. And I could understand both the delay and the surprised silence that had descended on the street when I saw Bhimanna's wife slowly making her way through the crowd. Everyone in Narasimhapura knew that the old lady rarely ever stepped out of her house. I wondered what had made her take this unusual step just a few days after Bhimanna's death and when the town was so tense. I got the answer soon enough.

'Who started the fire?' she asked.

I was perplexed. There had been a lot of fires through the night in Narasimhapura but I didn't know of any that should bother the old lady.

'What fire?' I asked.

'The fire the whole town is talking about. Everyone is saying the office was set on fire; that that woman Savitri and Krishnappa's boys got into a fight and set the paper's office on fire.'

'There is no fire here, amma,' I told her, trying to calm her down.

'Then why is everybody standing on the road. Why aren't you sitting inside the office?'

I was not quite sure I wanted to go into all the details of what had happened till then. The old lady's presence had cooled tempers down a bit, but the temperature was bound to rise if we had another public recounting of all the recent events.

'Nothing has happened, amma,' I said, adopting a tone which I thought would calm her down. 'If anything had happened wouldn't I have come and told you?'

The tone didn't really help.

'Of course you wouldn't. When have you ever come to tell us anything? You've always kept everything a secret. That is why he always made it a point to come to the office every day.'

I would have been less stunned if she had struck me across the face. I had committed my whole life to Bhimanna and his paper, and what do I receive in return? An insult in front of the whole town. All the work I had done for *The Narasimhapura Post* was because I always thought Bhimanna trusted me. The nights I had spent to ensure that the paper came out the next morning. Even now, after his death, I was so concerned about keeping the paper functioning only because I wanted to ensure that his memory would be kept alive. Yet all the while he had never trusted me. And, as if that was not bad enough, it now had to be disclosed to the entire town and a couple of eavesdropping riot-policemen who did not even belong to Narasimhapura.

I was completely dumbstruck. But even if I had known what I wanted to say, I doubt if I would have been allowed to speak. Savitri had decided that the debate was moving in the wrong direction.

'What is everyone talking about? Here we are discussing things of importance to the very future of Narasimhapura and we keep getting disturbed. None of us have time to waste.'

She then walked up to the old lady and said brusquely, 'Amma, you can see there is nothing wrong here. So why don't you leave us alone?'

I could have told her that that was the wrong tone. After what the old lady had told me I wasn't feeling too soft towards any member of Bhimanna's family, but you couldn't speak to an old lady like that. Certainly not to the wife of someone who had been one of Narasimhapura's best known citizens, a lady who had never acted superior to the rest of the town. All the years she had spent in the background were seen as years of sacrifice. There was no way that any young girl could talk to the old lady like this in Narasimhapura without generating anger.

Thimanna was quick to react. His eyes grew even larger and his anger made his cheeks flush.

'See, see, see,' he said, pointing to Savitri. 'Didn't I tell you she did not know how to behave? Look at the way she is talking to amma! Have we all lost our manhood for us to accept this? We will not rest until she apologises.'

The murmur of approval was loud enough for even Savitri to realise that she had gone too far. But then she was not someone who withdrew easily.

'What did I say? All I did was ask amma to go home and rest. After the ordeal that she has been through over the last few days it would be best if she rested.'

But Thimanna was not one to let go when he was on top.

'All of you heard her,' he said. 'Did she show enough respect for amma? She may be used to talking to people like that where she comes from. But we won't allow it in Narasimhapura. Our entire pride is at stake. Are we going to let this insult go unanswered?'

The approval this time was even louder, spurring Thimanna to greater heights.

'If people think they can come to our town and insult our mothers and sisters we will have to show them what Narasimhapura is.'

This time he was greeted with a loud cheer.

'I ask all those persons who call themselves men in this audience to come and stand beside me in this battle to save Narasimhapura's honour. Let us make it clear to all concerned that we are willing to lay down our lives to protect the honour of our mothers.'

The response this time was the loudest yet. Some of the men in Savitri's group too joined in the cheers. A group of men led by Thimanna started moving menacingly towards Savitri. Puttaswamy sprang in front of her. I don't know where he had come from, but the boy had begun to make a habit of standing protectively in front of Savitri. Pushing his skinny body aside wouldn't have required anything more than the brief attention of even the weakest of the group Thimanna was leading.

But fortunately things did not reach that point. The old lady moved between the two groups with her arms held wide apart.

'What is wrong with you?' she scolded Thimanna. 'What kind of a man are you who threatens to attack a girl?'

Thimanna and his about-to-make-merry men stopped in their tracks. This attacking-a-girl business had transformed them in a matter of seconds, from prospective heroes to likely villains. He looked down, unable to meet the old lady's eyes.

'And just what are you fighting about? Whatever the problem is I am sure there will be some solution. Why do you have to bring everything to the streets?'

I thought this was the appropriate moment to step in. 'Of course there are solutions. There must be plenty of solutions. Why should there be a shortage of solutions?'

'What are the solutions?' Savitri asked.

'Yes, what are they?' said Thimanna.

Their unexpected common stand unnerved me.

'When I said there were solutions, I didn't mean that there were already solutions. I am sure that if everyone sits down some solution can be found.'

'Yes,' said the old lady. 'Why don't all of you go into the office and work out a solution? I am sure Rangarajan will publish it in the paper tomorrow.'

'Yes, yes, of course,' I said before I realised what I was saying.

'Just what solution are you going to publish tomorrow?' Savitri wanted to know.

'Yes, we must know,' said Thimanna, sounding like the judge in the local school play. 'We cannot have a solution that compromises the pride of Narasimhapura.'

'Is the pride of Narasimhapura in destroying monuments?' asked Savitri with all her usual aggressiveness.

'Is the pride of Narasimhapura in not having the courage to build a proper temple for the local deity?' Thimanna countered.

This wasn't getting us anywhere. If it went on a while longer the calm that the old lady had managed to bring would disappear.

'There are always two sides to an issue,' I intervened. 'Why don't both of you write out your solutions and we will carry both in the paper.'

This seemed to please both of them, but they were immediately suspicious.

'Where will you carry my piece?' Savitri asked.

'And where will you carry my piece?' Thimanna wanted to know.

'You must carry my piece on the top left-hand corner of the front page,' Savitri insisted.

Thimanna, quite predictably, wanted his solution to be carried at the same place. Considering how much the two of them seemed to think on identical lines, I wondered what made them dislike each other so intensely.

'We will draw lots,' I said. 'Whoever wins will get the top left-hand corner and the loser can decide where he or she wants his or her story to go. You must bring your stories to me by this evening.'

Savitri and Thimanna still looked at me quite suspiciously but the old lady seemed to think the whole matter was settled and started walking slowly down the road. The rest of the crowd too seemed to think the show was over and slowly dispersed. With a sigh of relief I walked back into the office and collapsed into the old steel chair.

▲ 9 ▼

Years of use had made the old chair with the cotton cushions extremely comfortable. I could slide down and really stretch my legs, but I rarely had an opportunity to relax like this. I was usually rather busy or pretending to be busy if there was someone else in the office. And the noise during the day from the street outside made it difficult to relax. But today, there was no one else in the office, Puttaswamy having left with Savitri. With the streets once again deserted, after the two groups had cleared out, it was also very quiet. And as I reclined on the chair and stared at the ceiling, I found the simple pattern of the row of brown beams comforting after the chaotic events of the last few days. I soon forgot my troubles and even began to think of what it would be like when I had full control of the paper. It would perhaps take me a few days to get rid of Puttaswamy and after that it would all be nice and peaceful. The mere thought of such a future brought a smile to my lips and lulled me into a comfortable sleep.

When I woke up it was to the sounds of an argument. Savitri and Thimanna were sitting on the foldable steel chairs across the table arguing about whether the Res-Barki was, in fact, a monument. Thimanna was clear that it could not be a monument as the Archaeological Survey of India had not listed it, while Savitri was going on about how monuments were determined by some 'dialektiks'.

I listened to them for a while wondering why they hadn't left. But when I glanced at the old clock, I realised it was five in the evening. I had evidently slept for most of the afternoon.

I rubbed my eyes and decided to stop their silly argument.

'Have you brought your solutions?' I asked.

'I have brought some,' Savitri said.

'So have I,' said Thimanna.

'What do you mean, 'some'? Do you mean that each of you has brought more than one solution?'

'Yes,' Savitri began. 'Since most of our group had different views we decided that we will bring all of them.'

'Yes,' Thimanna said, 'it was the same with our group too. So I have also brought several solutions.'

'If everyone in your own groups cannot agree on a single solution how do you expect the other side to agree to your solutions?' I asked, I thought reasonably.

Savitri gave me a pitying look.

'When we say different, we don't mean fundamentally different. It is just that there is more than one secular solution.'

Thimanna seemed to agree.

'Our precise solutions may be different but they are all aimed at protecting the pride of the Old Residents.'

I didn't want to argue with the lunatics, so I just took the solutions from them and began to read them.

Savitri's first solution was attributed to someone in Bangalore who, she told me with the air of a school teacher explaining who Jawaharlal Nehru was, was one of the most important scientists in Bangalore. He must have been, because his solution seemed to have found a way of defying the basic laws of gravity. He wanted a temple for the deity built on the site and the Res-Barki mounted on top of the gopuram.

'Won't it fall?' I asked Savitri, having visions of innocent pilgrims being killed by a falling Res-Barki resulting in further riots in Narasimhapura. But all I got as a response was a trust-you-to-say-something-stupid look.

Her second solution, which she attributed to an artist whose name was evidently well known but has slipped my mind now, seemed more scientifically sound to me. It consisted of six huge concrete beams making a dome over the Res-Barki. The beams then extended to form a lotus on top of the dome. Narasimhapura's deity would be placed in the middle of the lotus.

The third solution she said she had developed herself, and I must admit that it looked it. It consisted of four people standing in four corners holding aloft a hammer, a sickle, a gun and a lathi respectively. The weapons formed a kind of shield over the Res-Barki and simultaneously held up a slab of concrete shaped like a cloud. And on top of the cloud was to be the deity.

Thimanna's solutions had no place for the Res-Barki. All of them involved building a temple for the local deity.

The specifics of the temple were also clearly worked out. It was to be big enough to cover the entire Barkisthal. It was to be centrally air-conditioned. It was to have its own power station and an auditorium with a seating capacity of 45,000. The floor was to be of imported marble and built into the idol of the deity would be different coloured lights; the eyes were to be green lights and the bindi on the forehead a bright maroon light. Over the gate to the temple was to be a huge arch with moving lights forming the word 'WELCOME'.

The only differences were on how the Res-Barki was to be removed. The more aggressive ones wanted to tear it to the ground while the moderates wanted to remove it and situate it at a respectful distance from the new temple. Among the moderates there were further differences on how the Res-Barki was to be moved. Some thought it was enough if the job was entrusted to a group of engineers, but the more pious ones suggested, as a gesture of goodwill towards the Barkis, that the Res-Barki could be moved respectfully with each piece being taken in a procession in a flower-bedecked chariot which would later be donated to the Barki temple.

I was careful to ensure that I didn't show any reaction at all to any of the proposals. I then wrote out the name of each proposal on a small bit of paper, folded the little pieces into even smaller bits and put them into my old tumbler. I then asked Savitri and Thimanna to pick up the articles that would go into each slot of the front page. As expected both had complaints about the format, but I had made it clear that the draw of lots was final. All that they could do was grumble, which they did all the way out of the office.

Having completed my work with all the professionalism

expected of a journalist of my seniority, I began walking home. As I entered Mahatma Gandhi Road I saw Krishnappa coming from the opposite direction. Our normal routine was to pretend we didn't notice each other. But with the streets continuing to be deserted this was not easy and, in any case, I thought after yesterday a new routine would have to be worked out. I stopped to talk to him, hoping to keep it brief.

'What is your paper carrying tomorrow?' he asked with his usual directness.

I didn't see how it was any of his business. I did not want him to think that just because I had accepted his request once, he had become some sort of a super-editor. I thought it necessary to make it clear that his influence was for one issue only.

'I don't think you will like what we are carrying tomorrow,' I told him. 'We are carrying an article by Savitri on page 1.'

'What made you do that?'

'Owner's orders,' I told him. 'Bhimanna's wife wanted solutions to the problem to be carried, so we are carrying it.'

'In that case, perhaps I should buy your paper.'

That seemed a pretty odd thing to say. I didn't know too many people who decided to buy a paper because the owner wanted something to be carried in it. And, in any case, I wondered why Krishnappa, one of our oldest subscribers, had to buy a copy so late in the day.

'Having problems with the delivery boy, are you?' I asked.

'No, why do you ask?'

'Well, you said you wanted to buy a copy of the paper, so I thought you had not got today's copy.'

'I didn't say I wanted to buy a copy of the paper, I said I wanted to buy *The Narasimhapura Post.*'

He said it as if it was the most obvious thing to do. And looking back now, I suppose it was. After all, who would need a loss-making local paper other than the local politician? But with all that had happened since Bhimanna had died, it had just not struck me that the answer to all my problems would be Krishnappa. It is not that I had any complaints about Krishnappa being my saviour. As they say, when the Lord wants to help you who are you to decide what form it should take?

The sheer joy of having found a potential buyer for *The Post* must have been evident in the expression on my face. Krishnappa took a deep breath and with a flourish took the towel he had slung over his right shoulder and put it on his left. As he looked down his nose at me it was evident that he believed he finally had me where he wanted. I would be lying if I said I was enjoying the new relationship. But I have always been a man of the world. And if my behaviour could help Krishnappa make up his mind to buy *The Post*, I was going to do everything to help. I quickly adopted a tone and posture that I was sure would convey the admiration of the weak for the powerful.

'What an excellent idea. *The Narasimhapura Post* could not have found a better owner. Your commitment, your power, your deep insight into the problems of Narasimhapura will all strengthen the paper. I happen to know that Gopalakrishna wants to sell the paper. If you let me take you to him I am sure very favourable terms can be worked out. After all, who knows more about the paper than me? I have given my entire life to the paper.'

Krishnappa must have been quite amused by my

sudden reappraisal of his character, but he hid it well. 'Well, I haven't decided how to go about it. But I will keep your offer in mind.'

I was not going to let him get away that easily. 'But you must come with me. I will be able to get you a much better price. Let me tell you something that no one else knows. The family is quite upset about all that has happened and is very keen to get out of Narasimhapura. They want to do so within a week. They are contacting possible buyers in Bombay. And you know what will happen if Bombay money comes in. We will hardly be in a position to offer a comparable price. But if we act quickly I am sure we can get it cheap.'

I don't know whether he believed me or not, but he seemed to think he had nothing to lose by meeting the family. I immediately offered to take him there the next day. He just nodded and walked away.

▲ 10 ▼

I COULD BARELY SLEEP THE WHOLE OF THAT NIGHT. FOR THE first time since Bhimanna's death there seemed to be light at the end of the tunnel. I did not want to think too much about it for, as everyone knows, when you think too much about a good thing it will not work out. But I couldn't keep my thoughts from going back to the possibility of *The Post* finally being sold. In my more optimistic moments over the last few days I had believed that somebody would finally buy the paper. But I had never imagined that it would work out like this. My initial joy may have been only because the paper was being bought; but the more I thought about it all the other advantages of Krishnappa being the buyer became evident. Unlike Gopalakrishna, Krishnappa had no great ideas about a newspaper. I was sure he would have no intention of making the paper like one of those big ugly things they have in Bombay. I could also not see Krishnappa getting along with someone like Puttaswamy.

The Last Post

With Puttaswamy no longer enjoying the support of the owner I gave myself about a week or two to force him to leave. All I had to do was get Krishnappa to shout at Puttaswamy in public and the young idiot was bound to resign. And screaming at people in public was something Krishnappa liked doing. The more I thought about it the more certain I was that Krishnappa buying the paper would not only save my job, but would give me back the authority I had before young Gopalakrishna got all his silly ideas.

The prospect of a return to the good old days left me quite excited. I can't remember when I was more excited about what would happen the next day. In a way I suppose I was as unsettled the day before my wedding, but that feeling was different. It is difficult to say just why it was different; but after all my years in journalism I have developed the habit of not resting until such puzzling questions are answered. The feeling the night before I was married was a mixture of hope and fear; in fact, a lot of fear. But what I felt about a return to the good old days had no fear in it. It was not also, I suppose, hope, as hope suggests some uncertainty. I had no doubt that it would all work out well.

Having spent the night with such thoughts I had no difficulty waking up at the crack of dawn, if you could call it waking up since I had barely slept the whole night. I went through my morning routine with all the care that the occasion demanded. I wore a clean kurta and made sure I switched my gold ring from my middle finger to my small finger. I had always believed that the ring gave me luck when I wore it on my small finger and didn't do it more often only because I had to be careful it didn't fall off. Despite my elaborate preparations I had managed to do it all far too quickly. I had to then spend most of the next hour pacing up and down the small path between the gate and the front door of my house, waiting for it to become a reasonable hour to visit Krishnappa. I must have made and gulped down three cups of coffee before I finally decided that I could wait no longer.

I set out for Krishnappa's house hoping that by the time I strolled there it would be a reasonable hour. I also visited the two shops, one at the bus-stand and the other near the temple, that sold *The Narasimhapura Post* along with cigarettes, biscuits, locks and everything else. But my excitement made my feet move faster than I had wanted them to. When I arrived at Krishnappa's place it was not yet seven. Having reached the gate I had no option but to go in. The huts down the road had been completely burnt down, but the site still had a lot of policemen around it. They would have been only too glad to question anyone lurking outside a gate.

Once I opened the gate I felt a little less nervous. The main door of the house was open, and as I walked up to it Krishnappa himself came out. The fact that he was all dressed up to go out made me wonder for a moment whether I would be brushed aside, but his opening remarks were friendly enough. 'Come in, come in, I was expecting you. I somehow thought you would come early.'

'Well, I didn't know your programme so I thought it would be better if I caught you early.'

'I am busy today, but we can finish your work first if you like. I have always found people are more reasonable in the morning before the world spoils their mood.' He roared with laughter as if his remark was the most witty one he had heard in a long time and, after a slow start, I quickly joined in. I had not expected to see him in such a favourable mood and would have laughed for the rest of the day in order to keep him that way.

We were still competing with each other in what was turning out to be a little laughing contest, when we heard a distant scream. The voice slowly came closer and was soon close enough for us to decipher what was being screamed.

'Krishnappa, Krishnappa!' The high pitch in which the name was being screamed conveyed a mixture of agony and fear. A few moments later the owner of the voice came rushing through the gate. His bare chubby chest and paunch were covered with sweat which made his holy thread stick to his skin. The tuft of hair at the back of his otherwise clean-shaven head appeared to be standing up in fear. The head priest of Narasimhapura's main temple was not known for his calm. Once when his young child had kept disturbing him when he was reciting the prayers at the annual festival of the local deity, he is known to have incorporated a couple of words into the prayer that were not there in the original. And those who were close enough to recognise the words, even though they were chanted in the same tone as the rest of the prayer, insist that they were words no decent man would ever utter. Yet I had never seen him as disturbed as this. When he came close enough we could make out that the sweat on his face was mixed with tears.

'Krishnappa, Krishnappa, Krishnappa!'

I don't know how many times he would have gone on repeating the name if Krishnappa hadn't stopped him.

'What is the matter with you?' Krishnappa snapped. 'What are you screaming my name all over town for?'

'Krishnappa, Krishnappa,' the priest began and seemed set to go on in the same vein when, seeing the expression on Krishnappa's face, he decided he would need to elaborate further.

'The deity, Krishnappa, the deity,' the priest said, as if that explained everything.

'What happened to the deity?' Krishnappa asked. There was genuine concern in his voice. There was not a soul in Narasimhapura, whatever his religion, class, caste or preoccupation, who could claim to be unaffected by the deity. There was no family I could recall in Narasimhapura, irrespective of their religion, who did not seek the blessings of the deity at the time of a marriage or when a child was born. Even Chikanna, the town's best known drunkard, was known to seek the deity's blessings before he had his first drink of the day.

'It would be sacrilege to say what they are planning. I know I have sinned many times but let it not be said that it was I who told the world about what they are doing to the deity!'

'Stop talking in riddles,' Krishnappa snapped. 'Just tell me who is planning what.'

'Thimanna.'

'What is Thimanna planning to do?'

'He is planning to take the deity all over town.'

'That little idiot! What would he want to do that for?' Krishnappa seemed genuinely perplexed.

'He says he wants to take the deity around Narasimhapura as a part of his campaign to build a new temple where the Res-Barki stands.'

'But the idiot can't do that!'

It was well-known in Narasimhapura that the deity should never be moved. She epitomised all the qualities of the ideal woman, including the ability to stay all her life inside the house without ever going out. It was believed that the deity had first appeared outside the town, though nobody had claimed to know the exact spot, until Thimanna had suddenly claimed, during that public meeting, that he knew the precise rock on which the diety had been found. Legend had it that, over five hundred years ago, the deity had appeared in a field outside the town and had then entered Narasimhapura mounted on a passing cow. The cow had then come to a point in the centre of Narasimhapura and had stood there without moving for the rest of its life. This was seen as a clear indication that the deity did not want to be moved and a temple was built for Her around the spot where She stood. No one in Narasimhapura had dared to even dream of moving the deity. And, since the temple was built around the deity, it was difficult to see how the deity could be removed.

A similar thought seemed to have struck Krishnappa.

'How can he move the deity?' he asked. 'It is virtually impossible to take it out of its present pedestal without breaking the temple.'

'Well, he is not taking out the original deity.'

'Then what have you been screaming about?' The irritation was returning to Krishnappa's tone.

'He has made a copy of the deity in plaster of Paris and is taking it around the city. You know no one has ever made another idol of the deity before. Even the most devout pilgrims have had to be satisfied with only a picture. It is against all tradition for another idol to be made and you know that the deity cannot be taken around the town like any ordinary human being.'

'I don't see what the fuss is all about,' Krishnappa countered. 'As long as the deity Herself is not being taken out why are you getting so upset? So what if it has not been done before. You, as the head priest, have always had the right to decide how the worship should be conducted. You can always change the rules to keep in tune with the times.'

The head priest was appalled.

'Krishnappa, you know me. I am not a man to stand on prestige, nor am I very rigid. I am more than willing to adjust to the situation. I don't have to tell you how often I have changed the rules to suit you. You know how much trouble I had to take over your membership of the temple board, when everyone objected to it on the grounds that you were not a brahmin. When you brought that ancient document to show that it was not essential for members of the temple board to be brahmins, it was I who authenticated it without even asking you where you got it from.'

'You don't have to remind me about these things,' Krishnappa said in a placating tone. 'All I request is that you help us out once again. I have also always made sure that you had no reason to regret helping me.'

'I know,' the priest replied. 'But this time you must forgive me. I can do anything with the temple or the rest of the world. But I cannot go against the deity Herself. My family has been Her servant for centuries. I will carry the curse of all my ancestors if I do anything to hurt the deity. My children will not forgive me.'

The fear in his eyes was unmistakable.

'I will not forgive you either,' said a calm voice from behind us. Krishnappa and I turned around to see his mother standing at the door, next to the green wooden grill. She had evidently heard the entire conversation.

'I never thought I would live to see the day when my

son would urge someone to denigrate the deity.' A note of anguish had entered her voice, and it grew as she kept speaking. 'When you were born both your grandfather and myself had vowed to ensure that you did no wrong. We thought we would bring you up in a manner that your goodness would be so overpowering that it would wipe out all your father's sins.' Her voice had now reached quite a high pitch.

Krishnappa tried to interrupt her, but she would have none of it.

'I have known for some years now that my dreams won't come true. But I had always believed that even if you weren't the perfect man we wanted you to be, you were at least not as bad as your father. But today it is all destroyed. Oh why didn't I die before this day?' Tears were now streaming down her cheeks. 'What sin am I paying this price for? Everything that I have ever wanted has been reduced to dust. Everything, everything, everything.'

As she repeated the word she sank to her knees on the steps of the house, crying uncontrollably. Krishnappa ran back, sat next to her and tried to put his arms around her.

'Don't touch me!' she screamed.

That didn't stop Krishnappa from putting his arms around her and holding the old lady tight.

'Amma, Amma, Amma,' he kept repeating as he held her. It was only when a son's arms had calmed the lady down a little that he spoke.

'You didn't understand, Amma,' he said. 'I was only trying to test the priest. You know what everyone says about him. I was only trying to see if he would fall to any depth. How could I do anything at all against the deity. Am I not your son?'

The old lady looked at him for a moment and then took the easy option of believing him. 'Then you must go at this very moment and stop it from happening. I don't care what sacrifice you have to make, but you must stop anything from happening to the deity.'

'I promise you, Amma, I will go right now and stop it. That boy will listen to me. It is just that with all this modern education he can't distinguish between right and wrong. Once I tell him not to do it, he will not do it.'

That was reasonable enough for both the old lady and the priest to accept. I was also sure that it wouldn't take very long, and in any case reaching the temple required only a small detour from the route to Bhimanna's house.

As the priest, Krishnappa and myself turned from Mahatma Gandhi Road into the road at the dead end of which was the temple, I realised, for the first time, why the priest had been so upset. The entire atmosphere around the temple was completely transformed. Normally, as you entered the road which was about 200 metres long you came under the shadow, both literally and figuratively, of the imposing gopuram on top of the gate that was straight ahead. The massive structure with Vijayanagara architecture was awe-inspiring and designed to make the most effervescent of Narasimhapura's population introspective. The rows of shops selling flowers lined both sides of the road. The small opening just a few yards before the gopuram was the lane that led to the Barki temple. The baskets of flowers on both sides of the road gave the place an atmosphere of worship even before you actually entered the huge gates of the temple.

But not now.

The atmosphere was anything but calm. A huge wooden dais had been built right in front of the main gate of the temple. The dais was situated in such a way as to block the lane leading to the Barki temple. The whole road was covered with rows of chairs. The flower shops were closed as all the flowers had evidently been used to form a floral roof over the entire road. There were bright decorative lights of every conceivable colour. The dais had strings of flowers forming a backdrop and a set of high-backed chairs which were also decorated with flowers. In the middle of the backdrop there was a moving light forming the name of the deity, and a foot or two above it was another set of moving lights forming the word 'WELCOME'.

If the lights were bright, the music was, well, even more so. It was so loud that we could barely hear ourselves speak. And it was, quite predictably, playing the unexpurgated version of a Hindi film song, which had had three of its lines deleted by a court for being vulgar. The opinion of their lordships was clearly not shared by the youth of Narasimhapura who always responded to this song by dancing to its beat with greater enthusiasm than an army man springing to attention on hearing the national anthem. The present occasion was no exception. One of the young men was dancing to its beat on the chair meant for the chief guest, with the crowd clapping and cheering him on.

The appearance of Krishnappa did not immediately curb their enthusiasm; but when the song was finally over they rushed to him with a garland. Having dumped the garland around his neck they cleared the way for him to get on to the dais. The young man who had been dancing on the chief guest's chair dusted it with his towel before offering it to Krishnappa. Krishnappa only patted him on the back and moved to the microphone.

'My brothers and sisters,' he said into the microphone and such was his hold over this group that he received immediate silence.

'My brothers and sisters, today is an important day for all of us. It is the day when we will show the world that we are worthy of our tradition. The task of protecting the self-respect of all residents of Narasimhapura has been thrust on our shoulders and we must show the world that this is a burden we can bear.'

One of the boys behind Krishnappa shouted, 'Krishnappa Zindabad!' and the crowd responded with loud cheers. Krishnappa held up his hand and after a while the cheering died down. 'My brothers and sisters,' he continued, 'Narasimhapura may not be a New York or a London but no one can say we do not have pride. And to protect this pride we are willing to make any sacrifice.'

The boy on the stage shouted, 'Krishnappa Zindabad!' once again and the cheers that followed were even louder. This time Krishnappa made no attempt to stop the cheering.

When the cheers did finally die down, he continued, 'When we launch a fight like this we must never lose sight of what we are fighting for. We are fighting for the tradition of Narasimhapura. In this fight we must involve all who are interested in the tradition of Narasimhapura. The head priest of the temple must necessarily be in the forefront of any struggle to protect the deity.'

The boy on the stage repeated his 'Krishnappa Zindabad' act, but the response was not quite the same. The mention of the priest had not been well received. Many of the young men and women present had spent most of their childhood teasing the priest and the prospect of their agitation being led by him was not very exciting.

Krishnappa must have noticed the marked difference in the response, but he continued as if nothing had happened. 'The priest has told us very clearly that it is against tradition for any idol to be made of the deity other than the original. It is also not acceptable that the deity or even a copy of Her should be moved around town. I have therefore decided that the idol that has been made will be kept in the temple and you can continue your campaign by holding meetings all over the town. If you want you can use a picture of the deity, but no idol.'

He moved away from the microphone with the air of a judge who had finished delivering his judgement. But the murmur that went around the audience suggested that he may have assumed too much. And soon enough a loud firm voice spoke from the back of the crowd, 'That is not acceptable to us.'

The whole crowd turned around and then gasped. There was collective surprise because Thimanna had spoken those words.

'What do you mean it is not acceptable to you?' The anger in Krishnappa's voice was unmistakable. I don't know if he had expected any resistance, but he had certainly not expected it from Thimanna. Thimanna was after all known to be a quiet, polite and intelligent boy who did what he was told. He was the last person Krishnappa had expected to stand up and shout back at him in a public meeting.

'I mean what I say. That is not acceptable to us.' Thimanna's tone was measured. He had clearly weighed each word before he spoke it.

'Are you defying me?' Krishnappa shouted.

'I have the greatest respect for you, Sir. But the pride of Narasimhapura and its deity must come first. The people of Narasimhapura must awake to the challenge that is being posed to their tradition. And if the deity is not used to protect Narasimhapura, what can it be used for?'

'But the priest has clearly said that to make a new idol and take it out in a procession will be against tradition and we are here to protect tradition.'

'We cannot protect tradition by clinging on to outdated rules,' Thimanna replied. 'If the priest had his way he wouldn't want women to study. His daughter was married off before she finished school. He will not want any woman to work.'

A murmur of approval went around the audience, especially among the women. The young men had been so boisterous that I hadn't quite noticed there were so many young women in the audience.

The muted expression of support gave Thimanna the confidence he was looking for. When he continued, his tone was more rhetorical, 'When we talk of saving tradition it is because we believe tradition will protect all of us including the weak. What kind of tradition will we have if we cannot help our sisters? Isn't the deity Herself a lady? Do you think She will like it if we do not protect our sisters?'

Then in a dramatic gesture he whipped out a pocket knife and nicked his thumb with it. He walked up to the white plaster of Paris deity and marked a bindi on its forehead with the blood from his thumb. He then turned dramatically around and said: 'I am willing to give my blood to protect my sisters' rights.'

There was now no doubt on whose side the women were. They all looked at Thimanna with awe. One of the more articulate women stood up and shouted, 'Thimanna is right, we must stand by him,' and all the women cheered.

Seeing that Thimanna had become an instant hero with the women, the other young men took little time to decide on which side their fortunes lay. One of the boys in the audience stood up and shouted, 'Thimanna Zindabad!' and everyone repeated 'Zindabad, Zindabad!' The boy standing behind Krishnappa led the next round by shouting, 'Thimanna Zindabad!' causing Krishnappa to blush.

Krishnappa picked the corner of his dhoti in his hand and stormed down the stairs. This was the closest I have ever seen to smoke coming out of his ears.

I wasn't too keen on getting close to him in this mood and thought it would be better if we postponed the visit to Bhimanna's house. But Krishnappa was in no mood to exit from the scene alone. It would have been the ultimate insult if he did not have someone walk out with him. He walked straight up to me and snapped, 'Aren't you coming?'

'Yes, yes, of course,' I mumbled and followed him out of the street.

Once we reached Mahatma Gandhi Road we both paused for breath not knowing what to do next.

'Should we change the programme?' I asked him. 'We can always follow up on *The Post* later if you are upset now.'

'Upset? Who said I am upset? You think those little bastards can upset me? There is no need to change any programme just because those little bastards don't know what is good for them. We will go to Bhimanna's house now.'

I nodded and followed him down the road, but I can't say that I was feeling light-hearted.

▲ 11 ▼

It did not take too long for my apprehensions to be proved right. Even as we walked towards Bhimanna's house it was evident that Krishnappa was in no mood for negotiations. He held the corner of his dhoti so tight that I wondered if his fingernails would draw blood from his palm. He made no attempt to avoid the potholes filled with slush. His long brisk strides and the swinging of his arms made him look like Ravana marching into battle rather than a businessman interested in discussing the price of a newspaper. As I walked a couple of steps behind him struggling to keep pace, I considered the option of drawing him into a conversation about *The Narasimhapura Post* so as to get him into the mood for negotiations. But at that moment he suddenly slapped the rump of a passing cow with such viciousness that I decided discretion was the better part of valour.

Krishnappa's mood didn't show any signs of softening

even after we had walked down the highway to reach Bhimanna's house. He pushed open the big steel-sheet gates, strode up to the door, removed his slippers, and walked right in. Gopalakrishna who was lounging in his father's rocking chair was clearly startled by his sudden entrance, but spoke politely enough.

'Krishnappa, what a surprise! Do come in. Why don't you sit down?'

Krishnappa walked to the old sofa and sat down stiffly, as if he was doing so reluctantly and as a favour to Gopalakrishna.

'Tell me, what can I do for you?' Gopalakrishna continued.

'You mean to say this fellow has not told you anything?' Krishnappa asked, pointing towards me with his chin. I cannot say I liked either the tone or the gesture, but I kept quiet.

'Well, no,' Gopalakrishna replied. 'Was there anything he had to tell me?'

'He has been troubling me, telling me that you wanted to sell the paper. He woke me up early in the morning, asking me to come and talk to you about the sale price, and you tell me you don't know anything about it?'

This was certainly not the way it had happened and I don't mind admitting that I was finding it increasingly difficult to keep my silence. Fortunately, Gopalakrishna replied in a more reasonable tone.

'Well, maybe he forgot. Yes, we were thinking of moving out of Narasimhapura and if you are interested in buying *The Post* we will certainly consider your offer.'

'What do you mean consider my offer? Do you think the whole world is lining up to buy your stupid paper? The only reason people buy your paper is to wrap up what they sell. Once plastic covers come here like in Bangalore or Bombay, who will want your paper?'

This insult to *The Post* was too much for Gopalakrishna to take. Whatever his faults, and there were many, he was extremely proud of *The Post*. When he replied his voice showed a tinge of irritation. 'Listen Krishnappa, there is no need to insult the paper. Since you have come here to buy the paper I am assuming that you are serious about it. Why don't you tell me what price you are willing to pay and then we will talk further.'

'Why should I give you any price? As if I don't know how much you are losing on the paper. As if that paper can ever make a profit. You should be grateful to me if I decide to take this burden off your back.'

By now Gopalakrishna had lost all his earlier calm. 'Does that mean I must give you the paper free? What do you think this is, a charity? If you are not serious about buying, why do you want to waste my time? If you want to pick up things free, why don't you go and beg?'

Any talk of begging would have been too much for Krishnappa to take even in his best mood, and now he reacted as if he had been struck across the face. He stood up and rushed towards Gopalakrishna. Luckily I was standing close enough to come between the two of them.

'Get out of my way you old idiot, I will teach this young loafer how to talk to important people.'

'No, Krishnappa,' I told him in as calm a tone as I could manage. 'I brought you here because I thought you wanted to discuss a business deal. And I will not have you hurting anything in Bhimanna's house.'

'Who are you to stop me, you fool? I can beat you up

so badly that your family would not recognise you. The only reason I am not doing so is because you don't have a family.'

This was getting too much for me to take and, for one reckless moment, I considered slapping him. His height and build stopped me from doing so, but I was seething with fury.

At that moment Bhimanna's wife walked into the room.

The entry of the old lady meant that the bell had been rung on this round. Krishnappa looked at her, held his palms together, murmured 'Namaskara' and stormed out.

'What is all this?' the old lady asked.

I looked at Gopalakrishna, indicating that he knew the answer and as he tried to decide what to say, I followed Krishnappa out of the house.

Out on the road the sun was really hot, or it may only have been my anger that made me feel so hot. It was not just the disappointment of all my dreams being so rudely brought down to earth. It was also the manner in which it was done. Krishnappa had behaved like the goonda he was. No one has ever accused me of being sensitive, but even I couldn't be expected to quietly accept insults like that. I had every right to respond at the right time, and respond I would.

My mind was full of such dark thoughts as I entered Mahatma Gandhi Road, and the scene that unfolded before my eyes told me exactly what that response should be. If the gods had been watching the events of the previous hour, they couldn't have given me a clearer signal. The road was full of people watching one of the most colourful processions I had seen in Narasimhapura. Having confronted Krishnappa on this issue, Thimanna had not wasted any time.

The procession was led by fifteen rows of ladies, marching ten abreast. Each of them wore a headband and carried a large flag. The sight of one hundred and fifty flags fluttering in the breeze immediately conveyed an impression of grandeur. Behind the ladies were young men mounted on cycles, riding three abreast. There must have been at least fifty rows of cycles. They were followed by a van on which was mounted a huge loudspeaker blaring the same song that we had heard earlier in the day. As always, the song had prompted Narasimhapura's youth to an impromptu dance. The large group of dancers behind the van created a festive atmosphere for the highlight of the procession, which was the plaster of Paris idol of the deity. The idol was mounted on a cart, pulled by one of those new Japanese motorcycles.

The only concession was that the motorcycle was made up like a cow. The two rear-view mirrors on the handlebar were decorated like a cow's horns. On the two sides of the motorcycle's crash guards were two pieces of cardboard purporting to be the front legs of the cow. The body of the motorcycle was covered with a white bedsheet and two cardboard pieces stuck on the two indicator lights at the back were supposed to be the cow's hind legs.

As the procession made slow progress down the road it was as if the whole of Narasimhapura had come out to see it. The younger children were rushing to join the rapidly growing group of dancers behind the van. The girls who lived in the houses above the shops on Mahatma Gandhi Road ran out on to the street, offering the processionists water and sweets. Older women knelt down in front of the idol, touching the ground with their heads, further slowing down the procession. Women with infants in their arms ran up to the cart and rubbed the kumkum from it on the foreheads of their children. Men of all ages joined the procession behind the idol, making it longer by the minute. At the very end were three truckloads of policemen, fingers on the triggers of their rifles.

The only people missing were the Barkis. The shops that they owned on Mahatma Gandhi Road were shut and there was not a single Barki in sight.

The procession was so impressive that there was no way it would not have been the lead story in the next day's issue of *The Narasimhapura Post*. But I also saw in it an excellent opportunity to get even with Krishnappa. I decided to carry the story in a way that would build up Thimanna's standing and highlight Krishnappa's efforts to prevent the idol from being taken in procession. Given the mood that was prevalent in Narasimhapura I couldn't think of anything else that would anger and hurt Krishnappa more.

I spent the whole afternoon with the procession. I got hold of Thimanna and got him to say a few things that I could carry as an interview. I had hoped to get him to make a more virulent attack on Krishnappa, but he would not go further than saying that what he did was right and he had no regrets going against Krishnappa. I, however, managed to get a couple of other youngsters to make the required provocative comments. One of them even accused Krishnappa of wanting to reduce the intensity of the agitation in a bid to find favour with some Barki women. I was confident that by juxtaposing these statements with the quotes from Thimanna I could convey the impression that Thimanna also held the same view.

I then went back to the office, wrote out all the pieces, and with the satisfaction that only comes from a job well done, I slouched in my chair for a nap. The viciousness of the articles wiped away not just my anger but also much of my disappointment at the possibility of *The Post* not being sold.

When I woke up I was able to look at the whole picture much more calmly. The prospect of *The Post* not being sold depressed me, but I realised the time may have come to begin to get used to the idea. I looked around me wondering how long this feeling of belonging to the paper would continue, and allowed my thoughts to go back to happier days at *The Post*. I was lost in these pleasant memories when I suddenly realised that someone was talking to me.

I shook my head and focused on the present only to see Puttaswamy sitting on the foldable steel chair across the table, clutching its seat with both hands. He looked tense and worried about something. If I had been fond of him I certainly would have asked him what the matter was, but, as it was, all I did was sit across the table and look at him.

'Did you see the procession today?' he asked glumly.

'Yes, I did.'

'Did you see how big it was?'

'Yes, I did,' I replied, thinking for the umpteenth time what an idiot this boy was. If I had seen the procession I would obviously have seen how big it was.

'Did you see the support it received?'

'Yes, I did.'

'Did you see all those women and children coming out to greet the procession with water and sweets?'

'Yes, I did.'

I was beginning to wonder whether I would spend the rest of the evening repeating these three words, when he suddenly shifted from an inquisitive mood to an assertive one.

'We cannot let this happen,' he said, gripping the edge of the table until his knuckles went white.

'Let what happen?' It was now my turn to be inquisitive.

'Let them destroy this great country,' he replied.

'Who is trying to destroy this great country?' I asked, as I was genuinely perplexed.

'The fascists, of course.' His tone seemed to suggest that I should know who the fascists in Narasimhapura were, but I was somehow not aware of them.

'Who are the 'fashists'? Do they live nearby?'

He gave me an exasperated look. 'I am talking about those who took out the procession today,' he said with not a little irritation.

I had never thought of young Thimanna as a fashist. Nor could I think of all those young boys dancing to obscene songs as fashists. I had always thought being a fashist involved greater discipline. But clearly I was wrong. Whatever Puttaswamy's many faults, he had read enough books to know who a fashist was.

'They are fashists, are they?' I said. 'I had always thought fashists would be much worse.'

'Didn't you find them frightening?' he asked. 'All of them marching through the streets today.'

'Oh come on, how can Thimanna and his friends be frightening? In fact, I liked the procession very much. There was so much colour in it. I have written all the articles on the procession for tomorrow's paper.'

I would normally have expected him to read the articles the next day, but since I was quite proud of them I gave him my copies. 'Why don't you read them and tell me what you think?'

He picked up the copies and began reading them eagerly. Going by the way his ears became pink and then turned into darker and darker shades of red, the articles were affecting him, though I was not certain he liked them.

'You don't mean to say you are going to publish this!'

I didn't like his tone. 'Since when have you begun to decide which of my articles are going to be published?' I snapped.

He made a visible effort to control himself and took a deep breath before he replied, 'I am sorry. I didn't mean to question your right to publish anything you like. I was only expressing my dismay.'

'What are you dismayed about?'

'You have glorified the entire movement. You have not pointed out any of the risks of the movement. You have not referred to the threat of a riot between the Old Residents and the Barkis. Didn't you notice that there wasn't a single Barki in town during the procession. Even those who have shops here closed them and went away.'

'Of course, this procession is a show of strength by the Old Residents. I am sure the Barkis will have their own show of strength in their areas.'

'I don't support the Barkis' extreme positions either,' Puttaswamy said. 'All I am asking for is a secular approach attacking the extremists on both sides.'

'Well, once both sides have got their positions clear some such approach is bound to emerge.'

'How can you be so damn complacent about it?' He

was beginning to lose his temper. 'Are you really blind to all the dangers of this movement? If both sides start taking extreme postures how will any solution be reached?'

I tried to calm the silly boy down. 'All negotiations have to start from extremes. Unless you start from extreme positions how will you know how much to compromise?'

'But who knows what the nature of these compromises will be? What is to stop the compromises from being very different from the ideal? What makes you think that a compromise Thimanna accepts will be honourable to the Barkis?'

'If the Barkis are willing to accept it, why should we bother?'

'What happens to the secular ideal? What happens to the ideal secular India that our forefathers wanted to build? What will happen to the secular Nehruvian ideal which has guided us since Independence? What happens to Nehru's modern vision of India?'

'I don't know why you keep bringing Nehru into this,' I told him. 'What has he got to do with Narasimhapura? Did Nehru even see a single Barki in his life?'

'You are missing the entire point!' He was yelling now. 'It is this kind of attitude that has always helped fascism grow. The failure to fight fascism in its nascent years in Germany led to millions of lives being lost. If Hitler had been opposed in time there would have been no concentration camps. It is not Hitler alone who is to blame for those lives, but also all those people, like you, who kept quiet in the initial stages. You must learn lessons from history.'

'Well, I don't know any German history,' I told him. 'But from all the history I know of Narasimhapura as well as my father's place, people have always fought and have always got together again. I don't know why you are making such a fuss.'

'You mean to say you are not going to change what you have written?'

'Not a word.'

'Then I am afraid,' he said pompously, 'I will have to submit my resignation. I cannot be associated with a paper that actively promotes fascism.'

I don't know what kind of reaction he was expecting, but I could scarcely conceal my glee. If I had known that this was all it would take to get the little idiot to resign, I would have done it long ago.

'Of course, of course,' I said. 'You must stick to your principles. Let it not be said that you work in an office that actively promotes fascism.'

I looked on as he wrote out his resignation letter. Then with a sudden movement he stood up, swung his cloth bag on to his shoulder and strode out of the office, without once looking back.

I suppose it was a meaningless victory as all my victories that day had been. I had got his resignation at a time when the deadline Gopalakrishna had given me for finding a buyer for *The Post* was nearing. Puttaswamy may have lost his job, but it was just a day or two before I lost mine. The joy of attacking Krishnappa too had to be seen in the context of losing the only possible buyer for *The Narasimhapura Post.*

As I walked home these thoughts weighed on me. It did not help that the streets were again deserted. After the excitement of the procession in the morning, everyone had decided that it was better to stay indoors just in case the Barkis chose to retaliate. The sombre mood on the streets reflected all that I felt as I left the office. But after a while my mind kept returning to more pleasant thoughts. There was the ease with which I had got Puttaswamy to resign. And then the subtle way in which my article had given the completely wrong impression of Thimanna attacking Krishnappa, without actually misquoting the boy.

These little professional victories made me feel lighter than I had felt in a long time. When I reached home I did wonder whether this would be the last night of my working life, but the overall feeling of elation was so great that I slept really well that night.

▲ 12 ▼

At the crack of dawn there was a series of loud, rapid knocks on the door. At first I thought they were rifle shots. But as I woke up I realised that the thought of rifle shots was only the result of recent events in Narasimhapura. Someone was banging his fists on my door. The banging had a sense of urgency to it, and as I kept listening I began to detect anger as well. There was an element of apprehension mixed with curiosity as I finally decided to see who it was. The apprehension was greater than the curiosity, and by the time I reached the door I decided it may be better to first peep out of the window.

The moment I put my head to the bars of the window I realised that my caution had, as always, saved me. Standing in front of my door, and trying to break his fists on it, was Krishnappa. His entire manner was far from cordial. He had folded his dhoti around his waist and tied his towel around his head in the manner of a man who didn't want to be encumbered during a fight. The repeated deep breaths that made his chest swell were evidence that he was agitated about something. And after what I had written about him in *The Narasimhapura Post* it didn't take much insight to realise what was bothering him.

When I say I realised what he was agitated about, I must not give the impression that I had expected it. Krishnappa rarely reacted in this manner. As you know, apart from the recent short-lived friendship, our relations had never been very good. He always had this tendency to get upset with me for no reason at all, especially over that little issue of land for the Senior Journalists' Cooperative Society. But however angry he may have been it had never come down to physical violence. The possibility of such a reaction had not even crossed my mind when I had written those pieces the previous day. Evidently the articles had been more damaging than I had thought they would be. Perhaps it had something to do with Thimanna suddenly emerging as a political figure.

But this was hardly the time for thinking about why Krishnappa behaved the way he did. Now that his mood was clear, I had to decide how to deal with it. There was little point in trying to reason with him. At the best of times he was not known to be very reasonable, and that moment was certainly not the best of times. I considered pretending I was not at home; but there was no lock on the latch outside the door to indicate that I had gone out. And, going by the ferocity with which he was rapping on the door now, he would have hardly hesitated to break it down. All things considered, the most reasonable course of action seemed to be to slip out through the back door. There was a little hole in the wall which was used by my neighbours' daughter when she needed to return home without catching the attention of her father. Her approach to the problem seemed worthy of plagiarism. Making as little noise as possible I moved slowly to the back of the house and then proceeded around it towards the point where the wall was broken. I concentrated so hard on keeping quiet that I put all other things out of my mind.

Which was a mistake. If I had kept listening to the racket that Krishnappa was making on the front door I would have noticed that he had stopped banging on it. I would have wondered what he was up to, and I would have been a lot less stunned when he suddenly appeared in front of me at the side of the house. If I had been less stunned I could have had a chance to dart through the wall and run on to the road.

Not that it would have been much of a chance. As soon as he saw me he showed a turn of speed that would have given a younger man ambitions of a career in athletics. With a few rapid strides he stood right in front of me and, without much ado, caught me by the collar.

'I could kill you,' were his opening remarks.

I couldn't think of an appropriate response to that and even if I had, I may well have been too frightened for the words to actually come out of my mouth. I was, after all, a decent man not used to such uncivilised behaviour.

'You think you can write any lie and get away with it?'

The fact that he had lifted me by the collar and dropped me with a thud as he asked the question made answering difficult. But I realised I had to at least make an attempt to distract his attention from the more physical aspects of life.

'I didn't write anything. I only wrote what people told

me. I myself was surprised at what Thimanna had said but, what to do, I had to write it.'

This time he lifted me even higher by the collar before he dropped me.

'Don't expect me to fall for all your scheming lies. I checked with people who were there when Thimanna was talking to you and they all said he never said a word against me. All that you have written are lies.'

'Lies, lies, lies,' he repeated and then slapped me across the face with such force that my glasses went flying and my thoughts went to the next life.

I had given up any hope of survival, when he, for some reason I couldn't immediately fathom, stopped hitting me. Without my glasses and sprawled as I was on the ground, I was not in the best position to make out why. There seemed to be a woman with a shrill voice who had stopped Krishnappa from proceeding further on his homicidal path. As I couldn't think of any woman who would come to my aid, I wondered whether I was hallucinating. I groped around and found my glasses. Mercifully, only one of the lenses had been shattered in its recent flight. I put them on and found myself watching an unusual spectacle.

Rajalakshmi was holding Krishnappa's shirt with one hand and hitting him with the other even as she screamed at him in a voice that was even shriller than usual. Behind her, and also screaming in an equally high pitch, were her three children.

Krishnappa was nonplussed. This was an unexpected development, and he was a man who disliked unexpected developments. It is unlikely that the sight of a woman and children would have made his anger evaporate, but it certainly didn't suit his political image to be seen doing the dirty work himself. He firmly pulled his shirt out of her grip and giving me a we-shall-meet-again look, strode out of the gate.

I struggled to get to my feet and with Rajalakshmi's help slowly staggered back into my house. I made her lead me to the large mirror in the hall so that I could see the extent of the damage. I expected to be bleeding from at least four or five places. To my great relief I found that apart from my torn shirt collar and the missing lens in my glasses, there were hardly any signs of damage. I felt like a truck had run over me, but it only looked as if I had been too hasty while dressing. Heaving a loud sigh to make up for any impression that Rajalakshmi may have got that I was not too badly hurt, I made her lead me to my bed. I was glad to note that the sigh had had its effect and she offered to make me coffee. After many years I had the luxury of someone bringing me coffee in bed. This was so overwhelming that it put all other thoughts out of my mind. I must admit that it was nearly an hour later that it struck me that I must find out what had made Rajalakshmi come to my house at that early hour, and that too with her children. And what she told me made me wish I hadn't asked.

'I have left Mohan,' she said simply.

'Why?' I asked, though I already knew the answer.

'He didn't come back last night as well, and I am not going to keep quiet while he runs after some slut. I cannot allow my children to be brought up in a house where the father has neither values nor pride.'

'But where will you go?' As far as I knew she had nowhere else to go.

'I will stay here, of course. Who else do I have in Narasimhapura?'

She said it as if it was the most obvious thing for her to

do, and for her it may have been. But what would people think of me? That I had lured a lady half my age to my house?

'Surely you can't think of staying here? What will people say?'

'What will they say?' she replied. 'You are like a father to me.'

'I know you think so and I have always tried to be a father to you, but you cannot just come and live with me.'

'Why not? Anyway nobody bothers about these things these days. Has anyone bothered to tell Mohan to behave? Has anyone supported me with him behaving this way.'

'But that is different. He is doing it on the sly. He hasn't brought her to come and stay in your house.'

These subtleties were completely beyond her understanding.

'I don't care what people say,' she said defiantly. 'As long as my mind and heart are pure, what does it matter if the dogs bark?'

I had seen her in this sort of mood before. She could be stupidly stubborn. If she decided that she wouldn't type out a letter one day, nobody could make her do it. But this was the first time she was being stubborn about as important a thing as this. She stared at me with such faith and determination that it sent a chill down my spine.

It was with an uneasy mind that I got up, changed my shirt, ignored her protests about not resting enough, and set out for office.

As I walked I thought of all the options before me, and none of them were encouraging. I could, of course, just throw Rajalakshmi out, but she was guaranteed to create a scene. The story of an old man trying to break up a younger woman's marriage was bound to be misinterpreted. But the option of allowing her to stay was not a very encouraging one either. It is not that I was very sensitive to what people said. I didn't mind being called names as long as it stopped at that. But to be charged with enticing someone's wife was bound to generate a strong reaction in the minds of people, especially when that someone was as well-liked in Narasimhapura as Mohan was. Now that Krishnappa had shown the way, there would also be no dearth of persons willing to give a violent expression to their anger. On top of that the possibility of having to suffer Rajalakshmi at home in addition to the office would have made stronger men than me quiver with fear.

Such thoughts had made my mood decidedly sombre as I approached the office, walking through streets that were still fairly deserted. There had been no incident during the night following the procession and some of the tension on the streets had eased, but Narasimhapura's residents were a cautious lot and were waiting for more definitive signs of an end to hostilities before venturing out except on serious business. The shops that were open had rolled their shutters halfway so that they'd be able to close it quickly if needed. The relative quiet on the streets made me even more depressed, but I was not to remain downcast for long.

As soon as I turned into Siddappa Lane, I was greeted with a loud cheer. The street was lined on either side by women carrying the same flags they had held during the previous day's procession. In front of *The Narasimhapura Post* a small dais had been created by bringing the rear ends of two bullock carts together. The bullocks were nowhere in sight but there were boys holding on to the front ends of both carts so that the rear ends of the two carts stayed together and did not dip to the floor. A loudspeaker was blaring the same, much discredited but often sung song which was rapidly becoming the anthem of the Old Residents. For a moment I couldn't quite make out what was happening, but the eagerness with which Thimanna ran up to me suggested something positive.

'We have arranged all this for you, Sir,' he said.

'For me?'

'Today's issue of the paper showed clearly that your heart is with the Old Residents. I will admit that some of the earlier issues had caused us some pain. But we always knew that could not have been your work. And the first issue after you sacked that communist bastard clearly showed us what you think. As a sign of our appreciation we decided to hold a special reception for you today.'

I was quite overwhelmed by this totally unexpected appreciation. I put my arm around Thimanna and led him to the dais. Thimanna got quickly on top and balancing himself on the two bullock carts which were not entirely stable, he launched into a political speech:

'This is an important moment in our history. The history of Narasimhapura will record that it was on this day that the movement of the Old Residents received support from the intelligentsia. Until now we were a movement of committed workers but today we have an important writer who has agreed to lead us. We have today received the intellectual support that the movement needed.'

This little introduction really touched me. I had never before seen myself as an intellectual. But now that Thimanna had made the point I did not see why I could not consider myself one. As he had quite rightly pointed out, I was a writer. And since I had come into *The Narasimhapura Post* as a young boy, I probably had more experience than all those journalists in Bangalore, Bombay and Delhi. The more I thought about it, the more I was convinced. I had always been an intellectual but it had taken Thimanna to bring it out into the open. It was like gravity, it had always been there but that scientist only realised it when the apple fell on his head.

Thimanna was now inviting me to join him on top of the dais. The two carts that made up the dais were shaking so much that I was wary of standing on them as Thimanna was doing with a leg on each cart. But the other boys realised my apprehensions. Six of them went to hold the carts steady and another two lifted me on to the stage.

Once I was on top, I had to decide what to say. As I was not used to speaking in public this was turning out to be more difficult than I had realised.

'Brothers and sisters,' I started easily enough, but couldn't think of what to tell this large family.

'Brothers and sisters,' I repeated, but still couldn't think of anything else to say.

'Brothers and sisters,' I said again, and this time I was determined to continue, 'you have given me so much honour that I do not know what to say. Such love and affection can only be given by brothers and sisters.'

Which only brought me back to where I had started.

'Brothers and sisters,' I began again, 'we are all one large family and we must all struggle and work hard to make this an even larger family.'

That didn't sound all right. There seemed to be a slight anti-family planning tone to it, so I decided to clarify immediately, 'When I say large family I am speaking in a general way. I do not mean that each of us should have a large family but together we must be a large family with more brothers and sisters.'

It was only after I finished that sentence that I realised I had once again got back to where I had started. But the crowd was cheering as if I had told them something they did not know. I decided that this was a good time to stop, and after waving to the little crowd with both hands I beckoned to the boys to help me down.

The moment I got down from the carts the organisers decided that the felicitation was over and switched the microphones back to the Old Residents' anthem. I was quite relieved that I had got off the cart before the song started because the boys who were holding the cart let go of it and broke into a jig. Poor Thimanna who had waited politely for me to get off found himself being brought down to earth suddenly as the ends of the two carts dropped to the ground.

I helped the boy up and took him into the office. Once I was back in familiar surroundings my nervousness disappeared and I was able to thank him profusely.

'That is nothing, that is nothing, Sir,' he replied. 'We always wanted an intellectual to lead us. In fact we all met this morning and decided to formalise your leadership. It was unanimously decided that you will be president of the Narasimhapura Old Residents Trust or NORT for short.'

'Are you sure?' I asked him. 'I have never been in this kind of thing before.'

'There is nothing to it, Sir. We will do all the work. All we want is your name. We were thinking of arranging a big rally and it would be nice if we could announce an important name as our president.'

I had hoped that being president would mean rather

more than just being a name, but the fact that he thought my name was important enough was quite flattering.

'Okay,' I said with the air of someone who has had responsibility thrust upon him.

'Very good, Sir, let us go out and tell them.'

We both stepped out with the air of those leaders they show on television who have just completed a summit, but the mood outside was somewhat different. The music was still blaring, but no one was dancing. Instead, they were all crowded around a police jeep in which Nanjappa was seated.

'What is the problem?' Thimanna asked as he reached the jeep.

'Who gave you permission to hold this meeting?' demanded Nanjappa.

'It was not a meeting. We were only felicitating our new president.'

'What do you mean it is not a meeting? Don't you know that the assembly of more than five people has been banned in Narasimhapura?'

'But we had more people in the procession yesterday.'

'That is the trouble with you fellows. Just because we allow you to do it once, you want to do it every time. We give you an inch and you take the whole town.'

Thimanna was quick to realise he was on the wrong track.

'It is not like that, Sir,' he said. 'It is just that we didn't think so many people would come, we just wanted it to be a small affair.'

It didn't seem to be a very convincing argument to me, but his pleading tone evidently made up for the deficiency in conviction.

'Okay, you disperse now and make sure you don't hold any further meetings without permission.'

'Then, Sir, we must ask for permission right now,' Thimanna said. 'We want to hold a meeting tomorrow to announce to the whole of Narasimhapura that we have a new president.'

'Tomorrow is not possible. I have already granted permission to Savitri to hold a meeting. I cannot allow you to have a meeting at the same time.'

'But how could you allow that, Sir?' Thimanna pleaded. 'She will say all kinds of things against us.'

'Yes, I know. I didn't want to give permission myself, but, what to do, she brought pressure from Bangalore. Her father is some big officer there, I believe.'

'Is there nothing you can do, Sir?' Thimanna's tone was even more pleading than before.

'I cannot do anything myself. But if you also bring pressure on me, I see no reason why I shouldn't give you permission.'

With that little bit of advice he asked his driver to take him back to the police station.

After he left we stood there for a while wondering what to do. A short while later Thimanna put into words what was going through our minds. 'We will have to go to Krishnappa. There is no one else in Narasimhapura who knows anyone in Bangalore.'

I nodded quietly. I was not particularly keen to meet Krishnappa again, but I knew it would be better if our first meeting after that morning's encounter was in a group.

A core group of five youngsters was chosen by Thimanna and the seven of us set out for Krishnappa's place.

▲ 13 ▼

A POLICE VAN WAS STILL STATIONED NEAR KRISHNAPPA'S house. But the tension had eased enough for the policemen to remain inside the van parked close to the place where the Barki huts had stood. They hardly noticed us as we stopped a while at the corner to work out our strategy before entering the street. Thimanna pointed out, and I readily agreed, that Krishnappa could be quite unpredictable. Thimanna had not missed the anger evident on Krishnappa's face when he had walked out of the meeting before the procession. I did not think it necessary to tell him about the morning's incidents, but the need for caution was quite obvious.

'We will have to give him something,' Thimanna said. 'Otherwise he will not talk to us.'

All of us nodded.

'But we don't have very much to give him.'

All of us nodded again, but Thimanna was not one to

lose his enthusiasm so easily. 'But we do have the movement.'

'But we can't give it to him,' I pointed out.

Thimanna's face suddenly lit up. His eyes became even larger than usual. 'Wait a minute. Why can't we? We can make him the leader of our movement.'

I didn't like the direction this was taking. I hadn't been president for an hour and he was already talking of having a new president.

'But if you make him the leader you will have to follow all that he says,' I pointed out. 'You will have to promise not to take out the new idol of the deity. And he may even give that priest a place in the movement.'

'No, I don't mean leader in that sense. We will organise everything. But we can make him the patron of our movement.'

'Will he agree to just being a patron?'

'Why don't we find out?' Thimanna said.

'Who will find out?' I asked. I didn't want to be the one making Krishnappa an offer he would love to refuse.

That set Thimanna thinking too. What was needed was someone Krishnappa would talk to for at least as long as it took to inform him that we wanted him to be our patron. We finally chose one of the young boys we had brought along. He had a pleasant smile and was so puny that Krishnappa would hesitate to hit him. And he was also a distant relative of Krishnappa's.

'Make sure you tell him that we are all sorry for the way he was treated yesterday,' Thimanna said. 'Then tell him that as a sign of repentance we would like him to be our leader. Only after he agrees to be our leader must you say that he will be the patron of the movement.'

The boy nodded intently and walked into Krishnappa's house. He was back so quickly sprinting down the road to the street corner that, at first, we assumed that he had been thrown out. But he was grinning. 'He says you can come in, he says you can come in,' he shouted as he ran over to where we were standing.

All of us then trooped in behind Thimanna.

As soon as Krishnappa saw me his eyes hardened. Evidently the boy had forgotten to mention that I was also with the group outside.

'I thought you said this was a movement of the Old Residents,' he snapped at the boy.

'Yes, Sir,' the boy mumbled, a bit shaken by the sudden change of mood.

'Then what is he doing here?' Krishnappa barked, pointing at me with his chin.

'But he is our president, Sir,' Thimanna said.

'What do you mean president? Do you expect me to be a patron when this son of a bitch is president?'

'Well, Sir, we needed an intellectual president,' Thimanna said in a tone that was a little too apologetic for my liking.

'If you need an intellectual, why did you pick up this snake?'

For a moment I thought Thimanna would say 'because he is an intellectual snake', but I had underestimated the boy.

'I don't think it is correct to say such things about him, Sir,' Thimanna said. 'We need the support of all sections of people and Rangarajan Sir has always been our supporter. If we don't make use of his support, how will we build the movement?'

'There are so many intellectuals available,' Krishnappa said.

'Name one,' I wanted to say, but it would have spoilt the image of deep hurt that I was trying to convey.

'But we have already decided on him,' Thimanna said.

'In that case I will have nothing to do with the movement. Even if you had picked up a passing dog and made it the president I would have agreed. But I refuse to be a patron when this snake is the president.'

My initial reaction to this outburst was anger. With Thimanna and his boys around me there was no reason for me not to hit back. I was just thinking of the nastiest possible thing to say when a brilliant idea struck me. It was really quite an outstanding idea. As it crystallised in my mind I realised why Thimanna thought of me as an intellectual. 'You say you will accept even a dog as president,' I told Krishnappa. 'Does that mean you will accept anyone other than me?'

'Yes,' Krishnappa replied.

'Then I know the person who can be made president,' I said. 'It is Rajalakshmi.'

'Rajalakshmi?' they all cried out in unison.

'Yes, Rajalakshmi. 'Don't you realise she has all the qualifications to counter Savitri. She is a woman, so Savitri's argument that we are male chauvinists will fall flat. She is more traditional, so we will not lose our older supporters. And as Mohan's wife she will prevent many people from blindly following Mohan into Savitri's camp.'

What I forgot to mention to them was that once Rajalakshmi was president, I could tell Thimanna that the pride of the Old Residents would only be protected if the president was given a house. Even if I failed to convince him, I was confident of convincing Rajalakshmi that it was her right as president to be given a house. And I couldn't see Thimanna being able to stand up to Rajalakshmi's tearful methods of protecting her rights. It was as promising a way as any of ensuring that Rajalakshmi would not stay with me.

I could make out that Krishnappa didn't like the idea, but there wasn't much he could do. Having committed himself to accepting anyone other than me, he couldn't now retreat. And Thimanna wouldn't have allowed him to do so. With Rajalakshmi as president, he wouldn't need to put up with even the token independence that I may have asserted as president.

'Okay, okay,' Krishnappa said. 'Now tell me what is your real reason for coming here,' he added with characteristic bluntness.

'Well,' Thimanna said, 'the main reason was to make you patron. But I will admit there was another reason too. We want to hold a meeting tomorrow and Nanjappa says he can only give permission if we bring pressure from Bangalore. We were thinking if you could...'

Krishnappa was businesslike. 'What time do you want the meeting?'

'Three o'clock in the afternoon. That is when Savitri is holding her meeting.'

'Okay. But you had better ensure there is a big crowd for it. I don't want people in Bangalore to think that I ask for special permission and I can't even get a crowd.'

'Don't worry, Sir,' Thimanna told him. 'If even a quarter of the people who came to see our procession come, we will have a huge crowd.'

As we trooped out of Krishnappa's house our spirits

were considerably lighter. The meeting was important for Thimanna and his friends to tell the world that it was not Savitri alone who could use mass mobilisation for her benefit. As far as I was concerned the thrill was in being involved in this kind of activity for the first time. I was quite excited as I drew up a plan of action. All the arrangements for the meeting had to be made, the next day's issue of *The Narasimhapura Post* had to be brought out in such a way that it would build the right atmosphere for the rally, and before all that Rajalakshmi had to be told that she had just been elected the president of the Narasimhapura Old Residents' Trust.

As I wanted to make sure that she didn't think it was just a ruse to get her out of my house, I convinced Thimanna to come over personally and make the announcement. I also told him to make it sound like a very big honour. And, at the right moment, I would add that a house went with the job. As things turned out I needn't have worried.

Rajalakshmi was sitting on the front steps of my house when we entered, combing her daughter's hair. I couldn't help noticing that she was using my comb, which no one had ever done before. Even my wife had had her own comb. But my irritation only made me even more determined to throw her out as quickly as possible. I nodded to Thimanna and he went up to her.

'We have come here to give you a very important bit of information,' Thimanna began.

'You mean Mohan has sent for me?' Rajalakshmi asked eagerly.

'Who?' Thimanna blurted. Her question had evidently not been in the script he had worked out in his mind.

'What do you mean, who? How many Mohans do I know. Has he sent for me?'

'Well, I don't know. He may have. But what I have come here for is a more important thing. We have come to offer you an important position that will influence the course of the history of Narasimhapura.'

Thimanna seemed quite relieved to get back to his predetermined speech. 'We have come here,' he continued, 'to offer you the position of president of the Narasimhapura Old Residents Trust or NORT.' The way he said it you almost expected to hear drums beating after he had finished.

Rajalakshmi didn't quite know what he was talking about. 'What do I have to do? Who do I have to trust?'

Thimanna was nonplussed. He clearly hadn't bargained for this when he agreed to inform her about her election. I decided to help him out.

'You don't have to trust anybody,' I told her. 'This is the body that will control the Old Residents movement. Krishnappa is the patron and we felt we must have somebody dynamic as the president.'

'Krishnappa! That scoundrel. You expect me to work under him after all that he did to you this morning?'

I was quite touched by her loyalty but it was getting to be quite counter-productive. 'As president you don't have to work under anybody. You are the boss.'

'How can I be the boss when you are there?' she asked.

'We just felt you would be better,' I told her patiently. 'In any case, I am always there.'

'Yes,' Thimanna piped in. 'You can see your job as representing Rangarajan Sir. In fact, we wanted him to be president, but he insisted that we should give it to you.'

Rajalakshmi looked at me with tears beginning to blur the devotion in her eyes. 'Sir has been like a God to me,' she said. 'Even if he asks me to give my life for him, I will do it.'

I stepped in quickly before the tears could become a flood. 'This is a very important job,' I told her. 'You must begin immediately. We already have a house for you.'

We didn't, of course, but that was Thimanna's problem. After the response he received during the procession, I was sure he would be able to convince one of the shopkeepers to give her a room. Some years ago many of them had built little rooms on top of their shops after one of them had managed to get a handsome rent from a medical representative who stayed for a while at Narasimhapura. But after a couple of young men refused to return the rooms even after they left Narasimhapura, and instead returned over weekends for all kinds of activities, most of the shopkeepers became wary. Many of them preferred to keep their rooms vacant rather than rent it to tenants who would overstay their welcome. In any case, I acted before Thimanna had time to think.

'You must move in there right now,' I told Rajalakshmi and turning to Thimanna I said, 'it is important to have our president well settled before tomorrow's crucial meeting.'

'But I haven't finished cooking your dinner,' Rajalakshmi protested.

'No,' I said, 'there is no time to lose. We cannot allow a small thing like my dinner to delay you. Thimanna will take you to your new house right now.'

Before she could think of anything else to say, I rounded up her children, and the few things she had brought with her, and opened the gate. She gathered her children, distributed what each had to carry, touched my feet, and they all trooped out.

It was with a great sense of relief that I went back into the house. The signs of Rajalakshmi and her family having spent the day there were visible all over the place. The kitchen utensils were scattered in different rooms. The children had evidently decided that they would make excellent substitutes for their toys. My bed looked as if a whole school of children had jumped on it and not just three. But my distress at such damage was completely outweighed by the joy of being alone again. I set about putting things back in place, and in an hour's time I was able to go back to the office to work on the next day's issue of *The Narasimhapura Post*.

I was very clear about what the issue would carry. I intended it to be a torch bearer for the Old Residents movement. And, even if I say so myself, I think it was. I had a banner headline saying, quite simply, 'A New Dawn'. I then put in a front page editorial about the need to shake off apathy and step out in defence of one's rights. I used two large photographs of the procession. And I had a large main article about how the rally marked a turning point in the history of Narasimhapura, and how those who missed it would regret it for the rest of their lives.

▲ 14 ▼

I REALISED QUITE EARLY THE NEXT MORNING THAT THE DAY OF the meeting was going to be even more momentous than I had predicted in my editorial. That morning, as on most days before the recent series of tumultuous events, I was woken up by the milkman. It had always been my practice to chat with him as he milked the cow in my presence. Over the years the job had passed from one generation to another, the present young man being the grandson of the old man I had first employed, but they all had one common characteristic: they were my first source of news for the day. By the time they came to supply milk in my house they had invariably been to most parts of the town, and anything they did not know by then was not worth knowing.

'There seem to be more people coming into Narasimhapura these days,' he began as he cleaned the teats of the cow.

'Yes,' I said, 'all these village boys don't want to remain in agriculture.'

'I mean people from Bangalore,' he said.

'From Bangalore?' I was puzzled for a while and then I smiled as I thought he was just having a dig at the large number of policemen who were in the town these days.

'Oh you mean the policemen.'

'No, Sir. I don't mean the policemen. I mean all those people who have been coming in since early this morning.'

'Why on earth should anyone want to come to Narasimhapura from Bangalore?' I asked.

'I don't know. But they say it is for Savitriamma's rally. I have never seen so many cars and vans before. At least half of Bangalore must be here.'

This didn't make sense. I could understand people being taken from Narasimhapura to Bangalore for a political rally. Krishnappa did it all the time. But from Bangalore to Narasimhapura? I was sure the boy had got it wrong, though the fact that he was rarely wrong was quite disturbing.

My curiosity over who had actually come to Narasimhapura made me rush through my morning chores and hurry to Sri Venkateswara Cafe for an earlier breakfast than usual.

I had barely stepped out of my house when I realised that the milkman had been, as usual, quite accurate. There were a large number of people on Mahatma Gandhi Road who clearly did not belong to Narasimhapura. By the time I had reached Sri Venkateswara Cafe I had been stopped repeatedly by people who slowed down their cars to ask for directions to the public meeting. As they asked their questions in a funny kind of Kannada, I made it a point to reply in English which pleased them no end. After three such funny Kannada-English exchanges, I began giving the directions to the meeting automatically, every time a car slowed down, and from their musical 'thank yous' I knew I had done the right thing.

As I kept repeating the directions though, I began to feel the first signs of irritation. Soon the causes for irritation began to multiply. Sri Venkateswara Cafe was packed. There were a large number of cars outside and barely enough standing room inside. There weren't too many places where you could have breakfast in Narasimhapura and the fact that Sri Venkateswara Cafe was the only one with clean toilets must have added to the rush.

I had never seen the hotel so crowded. With a great deal of effort and skill I managed to manoeuvre my way to the counter. As I always came there for breakfast and always ate the same thing, I was sure that once I was seen I would be given my two idlis and coffee. I stood by the counter, waiting patiently for my breakfast to arrive.

I stood there for about fifteen minutes without complaining, as the hotel staff were clearly overworked. They were running around barefoot, balancing trays full of plates and those new tumblers which gave you even lesser coffee than the old ones. With the waiters also shouting out their orders to the kitchen, there was so much noise that I thought it would be better to wait for them to notice me instead of adding to the confusion by shouting out my order. But when after another ten minutes there was still no sign of my being served, my patience began to wear out.

'Where is my tiffin?' I asked the boy at the counter.

'What tiffin?' he asked.

'What do you mean 'what tiffin'? Don't you know what I eat every morning?'

'You haven't ordered anything. How can I give you tiffin if you haven't ordered?'

This was too much. I had been coming to this hotel before this boy was born and had always been treated with respect. Even when I was a nobody, this young idiot's father had always made sure that I was treated well. We used to spend hours chatting about what was wrong with the world. Over the years the fact that I would eat here was taken as much for granted as was what I wanted to eat. I couldn't remember when I last came here and actually ordered something. And now this young boy, who I used to buy those little coconut sweets for, was telling me to order my breakfast.

'What do you mean I haven't ordered! You know what I want for tiffin.' I raised my voice and it was not just because of the din in the restaurant. 'The same bloody tiffin I have had in this place for the last thirty years.'

'I don't know what you did for the last thirty years,' he yelled back without batting an eyelid. 'And I don't care what you are going to do for the next thirty years. If you want tiffin you have to order it.'

And then turning to the waiter next to him he spoke in a voice that was meant for me to hear above the din. 'The trouble with all these old people of Narasimhapura is that they don't realise times have changed. If I was to sit down and serve them as my father used to, do you think I would be able to run a big hotel? Do you think I could handle today's crowd?' There was no way any self-respecting man in my position could have eaten there after being spoken to like that. With one withering look, which didn't seem to bother him, I stalked out of the place.

I went over to the canteen in the bus-stand on the

highway and ordered my two idlis. It was a place I didn't normally visit as it wasn't quite up to my status, but I was too angry to care about such things. By the time I had finished my idlis some of the anger had subsided and I decided to linger over my coffee.

I was still thinking morose thoughts about what the world was coming to when a scuffle broke out in the verandah just outside the door of the canteen. As I had come in I had noticed a group of Barki boys sitting on the parapet of the verandah, laughing loudly as was their wont. I couldn't make out what was happening, but the fight was evidently between them and some people who had got down from one of the Bangalore buses. The fight was brief but not brief enough to prevent a crowd from gathering. A large number of Barki boys were on one side and all those who had come into Narasimhapura from Bangalore were on the other. For a while it looked as if things would get really ugly, but the large police force in the vicinity moved quickly to separate the two groups. The mere sight of all the armed policemen with their rifles was enough to cool tempers.

When the crowd had dispersed I asked a waiter, who had got an inside view, what had happened.

'Oh nothing, Sir. Those Bangalore boys said one of the Barki boys had touched one of their girls. If those girls dress like that how can you blame the Barki boys? Anyone can mistake those girls in pants for boys.'

This defence of the Barki boys did surprise me as the waiter was clearly an Old Resident. But then I suppose it was not so much a case of liking the Barki boys more, as one of liking the influx from Bangalore less.

'Luckily nothing happened,' I said.

'Yes, nothing happened,' the waiter replied and there

was no mistaking the regret in his voice. 'If those Barki boys had a little more self-respect they would have shown those Bangalore fellows. Just because they come from a big city and speak English they think they can get away with anything. The speed at which those cars and vans have been coming in since morning it is a surprise that half of Narasimhapura has not been run over.'

I was evidently not the only one to feel the full impact of the influx from Bangalore.

When things had completely calmed down I left the canteen and headed back home. Thimanna had told me I was required at the ground for the meeting at two-thirty. So I would have enough time to cook myself a decent meal. After the trouble at Sri Venkateswara Cafe I had to work out alternatives.

I had just crossed the circle where the highway joins Mahatma Gandhi Road when I heard the screech of car tyres. One of the many speeding cars from Bangalore had hit a cycle. I ran to the spot to find it was one of Krishnappa's servants who had been riding the cycle, wife and child on the carrier. I quickly helped the mother and child up, by which time the servant too had got up. Fortunately, none of them were hurt.

'Can't you see where you are going?' I told the young man driving the car.

'It is not my fault,' the young man retorted sharply. 'He was the one going on the wrong side of the road. I was on the left side of the road and I was turning left. I had even put my indicator on.'

The crowd that had gathered around the car was not impressed. I am not sure if they would have cared for his argument even if they had understood it. This whole business of the right and wrong side of the road was not something they fully followed. In Narasimhapura everyone went on the middle of the road until they had to move to one side or the other because of a vehicle coming in the opposite direction. In any case, I don't think they liked the tone the young man adopted.

'Who are you to come and tell us what is right, I say,' said one of the younger Old Resident boys and the rest of the crowd, even those who did not understand English, agreed with him.

'Take the blow out of his car,' said another.

The crowd closed in and in a minute the air was removed from all the four tyres.

As the crowd moved in, fear was evident on the faces of the occupants of the car, three of whom were young women. One of the young girls who was in the back seat all of a sudden decided to escape. She opened the door and began to run. The quickness of her reaction surprised the crowd around her, who instinctively made way for her to get out.

She ran towards one of the policemen and though he may not have understood what she was saying, her gestures were very effective. In a short while the place was swarming with policemen. As they moved in with lathis swinging above their heads, the crowd quickly dispersed. But anyone could see that they were just biding their time rather than regretting what had happened. With all this excitement even before the two rallies started I was beginning to worry about what would finally happen.

▲ 15 ▼

As I reached the maidan on which the two rallies were to be held, I could see that the police had taken all precautions. The risk of some of the crowd breaking away and damaging the Res-Barki was not very great as the maidan was far away from Barkisthal, being on the other side of Narasimhapura, off the highway from Bangalore. But the police were clearly taking no chances. The entire maidan was barricaded with bamboo poles. The barricaded area was not as large as it once would have been. The maidan had shrunk after the neighbouring eucalyptus plantations encroached into the government-owned land. But it was still quite a large area. Two daises had been built on opposite sides of the maidan and there was a bamboo barricade in the middle that allocated exactly half the ground to each party. The entry into each half was through bamboo barricaded paths that began on the highway and led right up to the respective daises. The entry points on the highway were about a hundred metres apart, but there was little possibility of any confusion about which entry was for which rally. The Old Residents' rally had one of Krishnappa's bus conductors loudly chanting 'Krishnappa rally, Krishnappa rally' in the monotonous tone he normally used to inform potential passengers about the destination of his bus. The entrance to Savitri's rally was equally obvious because of the presence of several jean-clad youngsters who obviously did not belong to Narasimhapura.

Crowds were beginning to pour into both entrances. Thimanna had been true to his word. The Old Residents rally was larger than anything Narasimhapura had seen before. And judging by the way the groundnut sellers were converging on that half of the ground, the crowd was expected to become even larger.

Savitri's rally was not small either. Almost all the Barkis must have been there. And what she lacked in local support she had more than made up with support from Bangalore. In terms of numbers, the crowd from Bangalore was not too large. It was what Krishnappa would have called a ten-lorry crowd. It had seemed as if there were many more of them during the day because they had arrived in so many cars. But what was really impressive was the press contingent Savitri had managed to organise through her friends in Bangalore. There were a whole lot of people with cameras and there were one or two television cameras too.

The importance that Savitri placed on the people from Bangalore was evident. Most of the chairs on the dais were occupied by people who had come in that morning. The only resident of Narasimhapura there, other than Savitri, was Puttaswamy. I couldn't help noticing that Mohan was nowhere on the scene.

In contrast, our dais had no one at all from Bangalore. Krishnappa was there, sitting right in the middle. Rajalakshmi sat next to him with her thoughts apparently far away. Thimanna was at the mike urging people to come in quickly so that the meeting could start on time.

I could have told him he was wasting his breath. The people of Narasimhapura liked to do things at their own pace and were unlikely to hurry up simply because Savitri's rally was going to start on time.

Savitri on the other hand didn't seem to be bothered about whether the people had come in or not. She always had this thing about being punctual. At the dot of three she began her rally with everyone on the dais standing up and singing some English song. I couldn't quite make out what the words were, but I think it began with 'we shall overcome'. I tried to make out what they wanted to overcome, but I was not able to. I don't think the crowd, that consisted mostly of Barkis, understood either.

After the song, Savitri introduced somebody in pyjama-kurta to the audience. He was evidently someone big because all the cameramen rushed to take his picture. I couldn't make out who he was and judging by the reaction of her audience, the Barkis didn't seem to know him either.

He then came to the mike and spoke in English. I couldn't make out all that he said, both because of the distance and because he was speaking very softly. But from the few snatches that I could hear he seemed to be speaking about Nehru and about how one of the very fair solutions that Savitri had offered was the only way out of the crisis.

He was followed by a series of speakers who roughly said the same thing. They all seemed to mention Nehru and Savitri's solutions. A couple of them also spent a lot of time talking about Germany, though I couldn't quite make out what the connection was.

Savitri ran through her list of speakers from Bangalore. After they had all finished I was left wondering whether it had been worth her while to get them. They had left the crowd of Barkis unmoved. In fact, I distinctly remember the last few speakers had been booed.

The message finally did get across to Savitri, who then announced that all the remaining speakers would be from Narasimhapura. And to show her sincerity, she asked Puttaswamy to speak.

I suppose, technically speaking, you could say Puttaswamy was from Narasimhapura, but what he had to say was no different from what had been offered by the earlier speakers from Bangalore. He too spoke about Nehru, Savitri's solutions, and Germany, though he made the connection between the three seem even more remote. I was not at all surprised that the booing intensified.

It was then that Savitri decided to get really local and called Mohan to speak. As he emerged from the audience and climbed the steps leading to the dais, the audience appeared to become just a little less agitated. I thought this was something she should have done much earlier. Mohan was liked by everyone in Narasimhapura, both Old Residents and Barkis, and he would at least know what would go down well with his audience.

But the moment he started speaking I could make out that all was not well.

'Friends,' Mohan started, 'I wanted to come and speak to you. But now that I am here I wonder whether I have done the right thing. After all these learned speakers from Bangalore have spoken what is the use of listening to me?

After all, we are supposed to come last even in a meeting in our own town.'

He was clearly upset about being sidelined at the meeting. The loud cheers he received was an indication that many among the Barkis shared his anger at the dominance of the crowd from Bangalore. 'All these great men have come to tell us what is wrong with our town,' he continued. 'They have their own interpretation and we are supposed to listen to them. We all thought that the problem was one of the Res-Barki, but these learned gentlemen tell us that the problem is about Germany.'

He got an even louder cheer for this one, making it clear that they wanted more of the same. And Mohan was more than willing to provide it. 'These learned men say that they are concerned about India. But they have all studied abroad. Does any one of them even remember his mother tongue?'

The cheers to this were the loudest. A section of the crowd started shouting 'Mohan Zindabad!'

Savitri decided that she needed to get the situation back under control. She walked up to the mike and interrupted Mohan. 'This is not what we have gathered here for,' she said. 'We have met here to protect the secular tradition of Narasimhapura.'

It was now Mohan's turn to interrupt. 'What do these men know about Narasimhapura?'

'They are all learned people,' Savitri shouted. 'They are some of the greatest minds in this country. We must all listen to what they have to say.'

'Why should we listen to them?' Mohan countered. 'Do they listen to us?'

This simple logic clearly struck a chord in the hearts of

the crowd. An even larger section of the crowd joined the 'Mohan Zindabad' chant.

'Do these gentlemen ever think of us?' Mohan shouted. 'If you go to Bangalore, what do you see? Large hotels, broad roads and big shops. But can you hope for any of those things in Narasimhapura? All these gentlemen have big cars, can we hope to buy them in our lifetime? Savitri says we should listen to these people because they are educated. But have any of our children got the same chance to be educated?'

'No!' shouted the crowd.

'We cannot quietly follow somebody because they claim to be educated,' Mohan continued. 'Following is for sheep. We have our pride. We cannot let these people from Bangalore come and walk all over our pride.'

By now Savitri had decided that she had to stop this attack. She ran up to the mike and grabbed it from Mohan. 'We will not allow people to sidetrack this meeting,' she screeched in her high-pitched voice.

I could have told her it was not the right approach. Mohan had become such a hit with the audience that any attempt to cut him short was bound to be resisted.

'No!' yelled the audience and the chant of 'Mohan Zindabad' grew even louder.

Savitri's reaction to this was not the most prudent. 'You sit down!' she shrieked back at the audience.

Well, she had clearly underestimated the impact Mohan had made.

The crowd surged towards the dais. The VIPs quickly sprang up and ran down behind the stage. Since the only exit from the Barki side of the maidan had been blocked by the surging crowd, they ran along the barricade on the other side of the dais, until they came to the barrier dividing their half of the maidan from the Old Residents' side of the ground.

Thimanna saw this as an opportunity and quickly shouted into the mike. 'Friends,' he said, 'today we can see how the Barkis treat their own guests. They call them all the way from Bangalore only to attack them. We will show them how Narasimhapura treats its guests. Let us welcome them into our meeting.'

He paused as if he was expecting a loud cheer, but he was greeted with silence. The crowd was caught between its desire to assert itself against the Barkis on the one hand and the desire to assert itself against the influx from Bangalore on the other.

While the rest of us were wondering what to do, it was Rajalakshmi of all people who took the initiative. She had been a witness to the happenings on the Barki stage like the rest of us, but she hadn't been as disinterested as I had thought. The sight of Mohan openly clashing with Savitri wiped out all the distress she may have felt over the last few weeks. The picture of Mohan standing alone in the middle of the lion's den, stirred all the loyalty in her that had been dormant over the last few days. There was no doubt at all in her mind that her place was at his side.

She ran up to Thimanna and grabbed the mike from him. Having gained the mike she paused for a moment, not knowing what to say. But she quickly realised that all she had to do was to follow the Barkis' cue. She stretched out as much as her round frame would allow her, put one hand up in the air, and screeched, 'Mohan Zindabad.'

The Barkis didn't immediately know how to react to their slogan being taken up by the Old Residents' dais behind them. But once they got over their initial surprise they roared their approval.

Mohan's heroics on the other side of the ground had not left the Old Residents unaffected either. All the inconvenience that they had suffered during the day had developed into a stronger resentment against the influx from Bangalore than most of us had realised. And, all said and done, Mohan was, after all, one of them. Rajalakshmi's chant found a great deal of Old Residents' support. The Old Residents and the Barkis started competing with each other in responding to Rajalakshmi's slogan. The larger, vocal crowd on the Old Residents' side ensured that the 'Mohan Zindabad' slogans from their side of the ground were even louder than those from the Barki side.

The speed with which the two meetings had been converted into a single large one against the influx from Bangalore left the rest of us on the dais amazed. Thimanna was the first to react. He decided that he had to make an attempt to bring the meeting back to the question of the Res-Barki.

'Friends,' he shouted, 'let us not lose our direction. We must not forget the humiliation that the Old Residents have had to face at the hands of the Barkis.'

But it was in vain. I don't think anyone heard him, for when he went to ask Rajalakshmi for the mike she simply let the plump hand she had raised above her head fall on his head. And even if he had been heard I doubt if he would have got the response he wanted. The chance to attack the snooty invaders from Bangalore had united the Barkis and the Old Residents. They were now fighting for a common cause.

Krishnappa, the seasoned politician that he was, was

the one to take full advantage. Grabbing the mike he decided to ignite the tension. 'Brothers and sisters,' he said, 'all these people from Bangalore come and think they can rule us. Why? Because they know English.'

He instantly got the attention of the crowd. 'Yes!' they roared.

'But we are not bothered about English. The time has come to remove English from Narasimhapura.'

The crowd was now a mixture of Old Residents and Barkis, and both were cheering him. As they roared their approval to every word that Krishnappa spoke, he decided to go even further. 'We will not have any English in Narasimhapura. By tomorrow morning not a single English signboard must remain in Narasimhapura.'

The whole crowd seemed to erupt at this call to battle. But Krishnappa was not finished as yet. 'Friends, I am happy to announce that we have with us the editor of *The Narasimhapura Post.* And I am sure he will agree that if Narasimhapura cannot have English signposts it cannot have an English newspaper. *The Narasimhapura Post* must be destroyed today.'

I jumped up and raised my hand to protest.

Krishnappa could barely stop himself from grinning as he shouted, 'See, our great intellectual editor is himself raising his hand in favour of destroying *The Narasimhapura Post.*'

I sat down as quickly as I could. My mind was in a whirl as I tried to figure out what I should do. Even in that confused state I knew I couldn't remain a part of Krishnappa's rally. I got up to leave, only to be sent sprawling by a push from behind.

As I tried to find my bearings, I could hear Krishnappa

shouting, 'He is now falling at my feet to have his own paper destroyed. We cannot wait any longer. *The Narasimhapura Post* must be destroyed right now.'

When the crowd roared its approval, I knew all was lost. The mood in which they were, I had no chance of convincing them to leave *The Post* alone. And in any case, I probably wouldn't even have been heard in the loud cheers that greeted Krishnappa's battle-cry. The large crowd of Old Residents and Barkis pulled down the barricades and charged out of the maidan, united by a common hatred.

▲ 16 ▼

It was ten o'clock in the morning by the time I set out to evaluate the damage that had been caused to *The Post* during last night's riots. There was not much hope of the paper having survived the madness. The rioting had gone on till late in the night. The streets were now full of fresh police reinforcements from Bangalore, as the journalists who had rushed back the previous night had hit the headlines of the state and even national papers.

But Narasimhapura was more normal than it had been in a long time. Everyone knew that with the Old Residents and the Barkis having joined hands in the riots, the divide between them had been bridged. Till the next fight.

The office was a mess. Papers were thrown all over the floor. The antique typewriter had been broken. The old teleprinter was a mangled mass of metal. The printing press too had been hit repeatedly with a large stone.

But inside Bhimanna's office the main desk stood

untouched, its green baize tablecloth as serene as ever. I sat behind it and looked at the paper on the desk. It was the last issue of *The Narasimhapura Post* and its headline stared up at me screaming, 'A New Dawn'.

I must have been sitting there for a while when Mohan and Rajalakshmi came in. Rajalakshmi couldn't hide her happiness at having Mohan by her side again. He was a little embarrassed at the turn of events.

'We just thought we would pick up her stuff,' he said.

I just waved my hand across the room.

She walked up to her table which had fallen to its side in the larger room outside. She leant over, opened a drawer, took out a set of film magazines she had kept inside and they both left quietly as if they didn't want to disturb me.

I just sat back wondering what I could take from the office when I had my next visitors, Puttaswamy and Savitri. Both were dressed very differently from what they usually wore in Narasimhapura. He had on a very smart shirt and obviously expensive trousers. His shoes too gleamed so much that I thought I would be able to see my reflection in them. Savitri wore jeans and her flowing hair was let loose.

They both came into the main office and sat on the edge of my table that had been thrown on its side. They looked at me sitting at Bhimanna's table, through the open door between the two rooms, wondering what they should say.

'We are sorry,' she said finally, and she seemed to really mean it.

'We have decided to leave,' Puttaswamy said. 'We thought we should meet you before we go.'

'Where are you going?' I asked them.

'The US.' It was Savitri who replied. 'We have both decided to study further.'

'But can you just go to the US like that? I thought it was a more difficult and long-drawn-out process.'

'Well, we had planned it some time back, but it just so happened that till today the time didn't seem right to say so.'

'All the best,' was all I could think of saying.

Puttaswamy walked to an old cupboard and picked up a couple of books which he had forgotten to take that night when he had left in a huff. I put my arms around both of them and walked them to the door. This time Savitri did not duck and run away.

After they left I went back to Bhimanna's room and sat for a while on his chair wondering, once again, what I would take back from the office. In a sense it was all that I had, and yet none of it really belonged to me. But I knew I had to take back something, something that would not just remind me of my years with the paper but would also reflect all that *The Narasimhapura Post* had meant to me.

It didn't then take me long to decide.

I got up, folded the green baize tablecloth and put it under my arm. I went down, brought a bullock cart and had the desk loaded on to it. I then walked home slowly behind the bullock cart, stroking the green baize cloth. And, as always, it didn't fail to comfort me.

OTHER MANAS TITLES

BHASKARA PATTELAR AND OTHER STORIES
by Paul Zacharia
Translated from the Malayalam by the author, Gita Krishnankutty and A J Thomas (pp.246, Rs.95/-)

Paul Zacharia is one of Kerala's best known and admired short story writers. His stories move through a wide range of moods and themes from the gently mocking and teasingly funny to the reflective and even violent. This is the first time a selection of his stories has been translated into English. The title story 'Bhaskara Pattelar and My Life' has been made into a film *Vidheyan* by Adoor Gopalakrishnan.

Gita Krishnankutty and A J Thomas are well-known translators.

...These short stories aren't merely well plotted and finely crafted, they are slices of life.
—*Times of India*

Zacharia reveals himself to be an accomplished writer. Economical sentences, a biting sense of humour, acute observations of the Keralite's social world, all these are present in these charming, always readable stories.
—*Society*

FINAL SOLUTIONS AND OTHER PLAYS
by Mahesh Dattani
(pp.404, Rs.175/-)

Mahesh Dattani is one of India's leading playwrights who writes in English. This is the first time a collection of his plays has been published and it includes four of his outstanding works. Constantly open to experiment, the plays vary from pure comedy to serious psychological explorations. From the energetic communal clash in *Final Solutions* to the satirical netherworldly manipulations in *Where There's a Will*; from the poetic palimpsest of *Dance Like a Man* to the sophisticated viciousness of *Bravely Fought the Queen*, the plays are a rainbow of motives, emotions and situational undercurrents.

Dattani is an authentic contemporary voice whose plays are rooted in contemporary urban experience and yet have a significance which can travel beyond India's borders.
—*India Today*

Mahesh Dattani...one of India's best and most serious contemporary playwrights writing in English.
—*International Herald Tribune*

INSPECTOR MATADEEN ON THE MOON
Selected Satires by Harishankar Parsai
Translated from the Hindi by C M Naim (pp.198, Rs.95/-)

Harishankar Parsai was the doyen of Hindi satirists. His sharp pen relentlessly targeted the heartlessness of our caste-ridden society, the vagaries of bureaucracy, the baseness of our politicians, and all the vulgarities and little cruelties that go unnoticed in our daily lives. By turns gently critical, mordantly humorous and downright funny, Parsai's writing is a telling comment on the condition of man. This is the first collection in English of some of his numerous stories.

C M Naim's translations have appeared in many journals and anthologies in India and abroad.

All in all, Inspector Matadeen on the Moon *is a beautiful book to behold and to read.*
—*World Literature Today*

Parsai's canvas is extensive and being a keen observer of the world around him, the stories are a delight to read.
—*Business Line*

NEERMAI
by Na Muthuswamy
Translated from the Tamil by Lakshmi Holmström (pp.192, Rs.95/-)

Na Muthuswamy, founder member and resident playwright of the theatre group, 'Koothu-p-pattarai', began his literary career as a highly original and poetic short story writer. Impeccably translated by Lakshmi Holmström, this collection includes, among others, his famous Punjai stories. Unique and often surrealistic in content, these stories are delightful vignettes of village life, defined by an astonishing range of imagery that is as startling as it is fresh.

Lakshmi Holmström has edited the bestselling *The Inner Courtyard: Stories by Indian Women* and translated *Water* by Ashokamitran.

Muthuswamy is a demanding writer and his narrative style has an odd dreamlike, surrealistic quality.
—*Biblio*

Muthuswamy has been well-served by Lakshmi Holmström in what is easily the best translated book I have read in a long time.
—*Indian Review of Books*

VAMSHAVRIKSHA

by S L Bhyrappa

Translated from the Kannada by the author and Sushuma Chandrasekhar (pp.262, Rs.150/-)

Spanning three generations and varied nuances of thought and feeling, Vamshavriksha portrays the moral dilemmas that erupt in a small tradition-bound town in Karnataka when long established social patterns are questioned in the name of individual fulfilment. A sensitive exploration of love and loss, of tragedy and triumph, interwoven with spiritual, historical and cultural insights, the film version of this much acclaimed novel won the prestigious Swarna Kamal Award.

Eminent Kannada writer S L Bhyrappa has written seventeen novels which have been translated into several languages, and has been the recipient of numerous state and national literary awards over the years.

Brilliantly told, Vamshavriksha is a masterly achievement...The quality of the translation is remarkable...an extraordinary accomplishment.

—Gentleman

A PURPLE SEA

Short Stories by Ambai

Translated from the Tamil by Lakshmi Holmström (pp.254, Rs.135/-)

The seventeen stories collected here represent the work of the innovative Tamil writer Ambai. Over the past twenty years Ambai has broken new ground, both in terms of fictional forms and the courageousness of her subjects. She has been constantly open to experiment: her stories vary from gem-like prose poems to fantasy and surrealism and to realistic psychological explorations. Well-known translator and editor, Lakshmi Holmström, captures the essence of Ambai's writing for the non-Tamil reader.

Ambai's genius is for the telling detail, for a language never forced, never intrusive or jargon-ridden, always delicate even when tackling bold themes...Lakshmi Holmström's superb translation catches the pace and rhythm of the original.

—The Telegraph

Ambai's stories in The Purple Sea are boldly experimental, pointing to the real source of the best Indian fiction in the vernacular languages. She makes use of polyphony, fragmentation and multiple perspectives, and her translator succeeds in capturing her technical virtuosity.

—Times Literary Supplement

THE WALLED CITY

by Esther David
(pp.204, Rs.135/-)

Vibrant with the sights, sounds and shifting moods of Ahmedabad, the walled city of the title, Esther David's perceptive debut novel traces the rigidly circumscribed lives of three generations of women in an extended Jewish family in the city. Rich in observation and insight, and written in a highly individualistic style, *The Walled City* is a haunting study of the powerful forces that both unite and divide generations and communities.

Esther David comes from a large Bene-Israel Jewish family in Ahmedabad. A sculptor by training, she lectures on art history.

Occupying the intermediate zone between memoir and novel, this book is a celebration of the colours, fragrances, ritual textures and variously coded emotions of a vanished milieu.
—*Gentleman*

...a journey across a landscape of experiences. Rising above the story of her own family and her own people, the narrator becomes witness to the play of human lives.
—*Indian Review of Books*

THE LACKADAISICAL SWEEPER

Short Stories by Gauri Deshpande
(pp.214, Rs.135/-)

In the sixteen stories collected here, Gauri Deshpande probes the truth about women, men, their relationships, thoughts, frustrations, absurdities. With engaging irreverence, even indignation, she satirizes not only outmoded ideas and old taboos, but also the currently fashionable norms of political correctness. Be it with acid wit, wry acceptance or subtle irony, Gauri Deshpande evokes a parallel world of submerged emotions and invites us to explore the complexities of human behaviour. This is the first collection of her short stories to appear in English.

Gauri Desphande is a well-known writer and translator. Known for her bold themes and innovative writing in Marathi, she has published poems, essays and short stories in English as well.

Deshpande's strength...comes through when she writes with earthy honesty and intensity; when questions are not relegated to the esoteric, but met with a certain degree of immediacy.
—*The Pioneer*

...Gauri's stories make good reading.
—*Express Week*

SOJOURN
A Novel by Usha K R
(pp.182, Rs.135/-)

Sojourn relates the story of Neeraja, a determinedly cosmopolitan woman, who is forced to move into a small town for a brief period. Even as she tries to make her life significant in her temporary home, Neeraja finds herself grappling with Amrutapura—with its casually bigamous landlords, its Mahila Mandali and its pigs.

The novel brings alive the bustle of the town and describes with subtle irony the dealings and distractions of its people. Portraying both urban smugness and the sordidness of small town life, Usha K R's debut novel recounts the disquieting story of an awakening with a blend of humour and affection.

Fiction has been Usha K R's major interest. Her short stories have been widely published, and in 1995, she won the Katha Award for Creative Writing in English. *Sojourn* is her first novel.

Usha K.R. is a miniaturist par excellence...The rest of the world should soon hear about her.

—**The Hindu**

It brings alive an imaginary town with its flavours and aromas, and the sojourn there seems real and memorable.

—**Express Magazine**

THE COLOURS OF EVIL
by Ashokamitran
Translated from the Tamil by N Kalyan Raman
(pp.202, Rs.135/-)

Ashokamitran, winner of the 1996 Sahitya Akademi Award and one of Tamil's best-known writers, has been writing novels and short stories for over forty years.

In the stories in this collection, Ashokamitran arrives at a larger sense of the world through the trials and tribulations of ordinary people. His spare, lean prose seamlessly blends together his acute perceptions, his fine eye for detail and his laconic humour.

N.Kalyan Raman captures the nuances of his chiselled prose, bringing to sharp focus the quintessentially human characters that people Ashokamitran's world.

How Ashokamitran brings to us the everyday life of the underdog Indian in Madras!

—**Deccan Herald**

...The Colours of Evil must be read, for the stories it contains cannot be retold. That is Ashokamitran's genius.

—**Indian Review of Books**

For further information about **Manas** books

write to :

EastWest Books (Madras) Pvt Ltd
62-A, Ormes Road, Kilpauk
Chennai - 600 010.